She'd fal[...]k

A handsome, sexy, charming jerk, but a jerk all the same. Paige blamed herself for indulging in a whirlwind romance. For agreeing to marry a man she'd known for barely a month. For letting him break her heart.

She blamed Alex for everything else, though. The cowardly way he'd run off before the wedding. All the silly hype that had followed. But most of all, she blamed him for the way he'd made her doubt herself.

So it was time to put him in the past, once and for all. Carefully pulling her chain over her head, Paige undid the clasp and a diamond ring fell into her palm. The platinum band glistened in the waning sunlight. She closed her fist around it...then hurled it over the balcony. "Goodbye, Alex."

She leaned over the railing to watch the ring fly through the air. It bounced down the sidewalk several feet before she finally lost sight of it.

Gone forever. Just like Alex. A perfect ending to what she'd once believed was a perfect love.

Paige headed for the door, ready to step into her new life...and saw Alex Mack standing on the other side.

"Hi, honey," he said with a sheepish grin. "I'm home."

Dear Reader,

Most women have had one, at one time or another—
an unforgettable love affair with a sexy, irresistible guy
who steals their heart...and then steals away. But what
would you do if that man came back? Would you let
him in, or would you barricade the door?

Paige Hanover not only remembers the man who
left her at the altar, she's ready for him when he
makes the mistake of coming back. She wants revenge
on Alex Mackopoulos for romancing her under false
pretenses—and under a phony name! Alex says he's
willing to do almost anything to make her love him
again. Anything...except tell her the truth.

I hope you enjoy Alex and Paige's story. It's set in
San Francisco, which was voted one of the sexiest
cities in America on the SINGLE IN THE CITY Web site.
You can find even more information about this popular
Temptation miniseries at www.singleinthecity.org.
And be sure to watch for Cara Summers's *Flirting
with Temptation*, the final SINGLE IN THE CITY
book, available next month.

All my best,

Kristin Gabriel

The SINGLE IN THE CITY miniseries

Kristin Gabriel
Engaging Alex

HARLEQUIN®

TORONTO • NEW YORK • LONDON
AMSTERDAM • PARIS • SYDNEY • HAMBURG
STOCKHOLM • ATHENS • TOKYO • MILAN • MADRID
PRAGUE • WARSAW • BUDAPEST • AUCKLAND

For Ann Auten—thanks for the party!

ISBN 0-373-69132-7

ENGAGING ALEX

Copyright © 2003 by Kristin Eckhardt.

This edition published by arrangement with Harlequin Books S.A.

Visit us at www.eHarlequin.com

Printed in U.S.A.

1

PAIGE HANOVER realized too late that she should have worn black sackcloth to celebrate her first wedding anniversary. Although it wasn't *technically* her anniversary. After all, her fiancé, Alex Mack, had left her high and dry before the ceremony exactly one year ago today.

Now as she stood in the rain looking up at the old Victorian house that had been renovated into a four-unit apartment building, Paige could feel her new red leather pants literally shrinking onto her legs. Already skintight when dry, the pants would probably shut off her blood circulation before long.

She stepped forward to rap on the solid front door again, then peered through the ornate glass sidelight. A doorman sat with his back to her, totally engrossed in a television program on the small set in front of him. She could collapse from lack of blood flow to the brain and he probably wouldn't even notice her on the doorstep for hours. Not that Paige needed a man to rescue her—not anymore.

Twisting the antique brass knob in her hand, she was surprised to hear it click open. Paige stepped into the foyer, dripping rainwater onto the clean tile floor. The doorman didn't even flinch at her arrival. His gaze was firmly fixed on the screen that flickered in the gloomy light.

So the place wasn't exactly a bastion of security. Paige didn't plan to stay long anyway. But when she saw the program he was watching on television, she almost considered running back out into the downpour and forgetting this whole crazy idea.

She saw herself on the screen trying to escape a tenacious reporter who kept thrusting a microphone under her chin as she tried to hurry down the narrow sidewalk.

"Do you believe in UFO abductions?"

"No," she said tersely, her eyes straight-ahead as she walked.

"Then how can you explain your fiancé's sudden disappearance on the day of your wedding? Or the fact that his whereabouts are unknown?"

"No comment," she clipped, before hastily ducking into a doorway.

The male reporter turned to the camera and spoke in a solemn tone. "One year ago today, this San Francisco woman woke up on her wedding day to discover that her fiancé had mysteriously disappeared. In our special edition of *UFO Watch*, we will hear why her mother believes aliens may be involved. And discuss why this left-behind bride is afraid to talk. Is the government responsible for silencing her? Or is it simply fear of the aliens that may have absconded with the love of her life?"

The reporter cleared his throat. "This is Cleo Dimont asking you to stay tuned and to always keep an eye on the sky."

The doorman shook his head as the program went to commercial. "Amazing."

"Pathetic," Paige countered, feathering her fingers through her short curls.

The doorman jumped at the sound of her voice, whirling around as he clutched his slim hand to his chest. "You shouldn't sneak up on a person like that! Especially a person watching a show about alien abductions."

"I'm sorry. I didn't mean to scare you."

"I wasn't scared," he countered. "I have black belts in karate and judo. You could have been seriously injured."

"Too bad you weren't around when that *UFO Watch* reporter pounced on me outside my house last week."

The doorman blinked, looked at the television, then back at Paige. "I don't believe it! You're her. You're the Left-Behind Bride!"

She clenched her teeth at the moniker the show had given her. Not that many people watched it among the hundreds of other local cable shows available. Still, she didn't like having her private life beamed down from a satellite in the sky for public viewing.

That's what she called alien abduction.

"My fiancé was *not* abducted by a UFO," Paige told the doorman, a story she'd repeated too many times to remember. "He just got cold feet. But that's not what the reporter wanted to hear."

The doorman nodded in sympathy. "Reporters can be pests. At least he was cute."

Paige hadn't noticed. She'd spent the last year avoiding any man who looked in her direction. But that was about to change. No more hiding from life. From love. It was time to forget about Alex Mack once and for all. To say a final goodbye to the happily ever after fantasy that she'd clung to for far too long.

That's why she was here tonight.

"I'm looking for Franco Rossi," she said, aware that a small puddle had formed on the floor around her.

The doorman grinned. "That's me. You must be here about the apartment."

Paige nodded, setting down the grocery bag she'd been holding. "I'm Paige Hanover. We spoke yesterday on the telephone." She didn't tell him she'd called as soon as she'd seen the For Rent sign in the apartment window.

The timing couldn't be more perfect. Her mother had called it cosmic fate, though Paige tried not to encourage Margo Weaver's increasing fascination with extraterrestrial life. It had gotten worse since Paige's stepfather had disappeared from the Weaver home a year and a half ago. Even Paige had to admit his middle-of-the-night vanishing act was strange. Almost tailor-made for a show like *UFO Watch*.

Like mother, like daughter.

Only Paige didn't believe in UFOs, alien abductions, little green men or any of that other nonsense. She cringed at sensationalistic shows like *UFO Watch*, hating the fact that she was now one of their subjects.

Paige simply believed that she'd picked the wrong man, just like her mother. But that didn't mean they should give up. Or cling to some ridiculous theory about aliens abducting the men they loved. It was time to face reality.

That's why she was here tonight. To prove to herself and to her mother that it was a mistake to hold on to the past. Renting this apartment was her first step toward moving into the future.

Even the unusual lease fit Paige's purpose. It was a time-share, allowing her to use the apartment just two days out of the week—Friday and Saturday. She'd paid the required minimum of one month's rent, though she'd have no reason to return after tonight. She would consider the extra expense well-spent if it would get Alex Mack out of her head—and her heart—once and for all.

"The place is already furnished," Franco said, "courtesy of my ex-boyfriend, Marlon. He owns prime real estate all over the country. I lived with him in New York City until we broke up, then I won this apartment in a landmark palimony suit and moved to San Francisco."

Paige looked around the foyer. "Was working as the building's doorman part of the agreement?"

Franco smiled. "It's more of a volunteer position. I'm writing my first screenplay and I thought this would be a great opportunity to meet a lot of different people for character sketches. People like you."

"So you don't actually live here?" Paige asked, still somewhat confused.

Franco leaned closer and whispered. "Don't tell anyone, but I've turned the janitor's room in the basement into my own little home away from home. It's absolutely horrid, but writers are supposed to suffer for their craft. And the money I collect from leasing the apartment will help me produce my screenplay."

At least her rent payment was going to a worthwhile cause. "Well, good luck."

"Thanks." Franco reached into his pocket. "Here's the key to the apartment. You have to furnish your own linens, as I told you on the phone. But you're welcome to use any of the CDs in the stereo. I highly recommend the *Wizard of Oz* soundtrack. You just can't beat Judy Garland."

Paige nodded as she took the key, not bothering to tell him that she'd brought a CD of her own. One that fit the occasion perfectly.

Franco crossed his arms across his narrow chest as he looked her up and down. "You look a lot different than you did on television."

"I cut my hair." She reached up to touch the damp fringe at her neck. The stylist had tried to talk her out of cutting her waist-length hair, but Paige was determined to make some changes in her life. Big changes.

Franco nodded with approval. "It looks good. Great outfit, too."

Paige glanced down at her red halter top and matching leather pants, still unable to believe she'd bought something this outrageous—much less put it on. Thanks to the rain, she just hoped she could get it off.

"The forecast was sunny and warm when I left home this morning," she explained, though she usually didn't forget her umbrella. She'd obviously had too many other things on her mind today.

"I hope it's not ruined," Franco commiserated, his gaze on her leather pants. "You should probably take them off and lay them out to dry." He opened a closet door behind him and reached inside. "Here, you can borrow this to wear in the meantime."

She saw him pull out a hanger with a black skirt hanging from it. "Thanks, but I couldn't possibly—"

"Please take it," Franco insisted, shoving it into her hands. "I don't want you sitting on my furniture in wet pants. Besides, it's a great skirt." He glanced down at the bottle of wine in her bag. "Men love it."

Paige transferred the hanger to her other hand, then picked up the bag off the floor and headed for the staircase. "Thanks for lending me the skirt. I owe you."

"Believe me, it's my pleasure," Franco called after her. "Apartment 2B is on the left at the top of the stairs. I'll be happy to show you the way."

"That's all right," she assured him, taking a deep breath as she started up the steps. "I already know it."

TWENTY MINUTES LATER, Paige had her leather pants off and the borrowed black skirt on, somewhat surprised at how well it fit. She thought it a little strange that the doorman would have a spare skirt in the closet, but everything about Franco seemed a little strange.

Peeling those shrunken leather pants off had been an arduous process, but definitely worth it. The silky fabric of the short skirt whispered against her bare thighs and made her want to sway to the Frank Sinatra song playing on the stereo. The song Alex used to sing in her ear when they danced. At least hearing it didn't make her cry anymore.

The rain had finally abated, so Paige opened the balcony doors to let some fresh air into the stale apartment. It was located at the back of the old Victorian. She stepped out onto the balcony to see the row of Painted Ladies, the nickname given to Victorian houses adorned with several shades of coordinating paint, across the street. Many of the houses were in various stages of renovation.

She could smell a hint of the ocean as the breeze picked up. Turning back into the apartment, her gaze moved slowly over the table she'd set so meticulously.

There were two plates with chocolate éclairs on them, the dessert she and Alex had shared on their first date. A bottle of premium champagne chilling in an ice bucket, the same brand Alex had purchased the day of their engagement. A dried arrangement of white gardenias and stephanotis in the center of the table—her wedding bouquet.

A ripple of apprehension fluttered through her. This was a big step in her life. Paige had spent the past year preparing herself for this moment. Telling herself that it was time to move on. But was she really ready to forget about Alex—forever?

Yes.

She took a determined step toward the table and picked up the folded sheet of paper lying there. Alex's marriage proposal—sent via e-mail over a year ago. Paige had been stunned when she'd opened it. Hadn't really believed it until she'd printed it out in black and white. Now her gaze flew over the words she'd memorized long ago. Words that were imprinted on her heart.

> Paige,
> We've only known each other a few weeks, but I think I fell in love with you the moment we met. Say you'll marry me and be mine forever.
>   Alex

She took a deep breath, then held the paper over the candle, letting the flame lick at the edges until it caught. The corner of the paper turned black and began curling toward her palm. She dropped it in a crystal bowl and watched it burn until it was nothing but ashes.

Then she picked up the imported champagne bottle and poured both flutes full of the sparkling wine. "Here's to you, Alex Mack." She raised one glass high in the air. "May you rot in hell."

Paige caught her reflection in the antique wall mirror, still surprised by the woman she saw there. Her thick brown hair was now short and sassy, tapered at her neck and streaked with auburn highlights.

She'd gone on a shopping spree, too, buying outfits like the slinky halter top and matching red leather pants she'd worn here tonight. No more shapeless linen shifts and boring pantsuits for the new Paige Hanover.

It was time for a fresh start, symbolized by the anemone tattoo on her ankle. In the language of flowers, anemones stood for anticipation. Paige had grown up with flowers, working in her paternal grandfather's flower shop, Bay Bouquets, then inheriting it from him after his death five years ago.

Now she designed custom floral arrangements for the homes and businesses of some of the wealthiest citizens of San Francisco. Her mother ran the front of the store and her stepfather had made all the deliveries until his sudden disappearance eighteen months ago.

Bay Bouquets was definitely a family affair, but maybe it was time to expand. Once she put Alex behind her, she could concentrate fully on her business. Maybe even look into starting a franchise.

But first things first.

Paige walked over to the stereo and ejected the Sinatra CD, then stepped out onto the balcony. Lights shone in the houses around her and she knew families were sitting down to dinner together. Couples were telling each other about their day. She'd dreamed of doing the same with Alex in this very apartment.

A dream that had been hard to let go—until tonight.

Holding the CD in her hand like a Frisbee, she flipped her wrist and sent it spinning into the night. "Goodbye, Frank."

Then her hand went to the engagement ring she kept on a chain around her neck. She'd worn it next to her heart for the past year. An exquisite half-carat diamond that had been a symbol of Alex's commitment—until her handsome fiancé had disappeared without any explanation.

Her throat tightened, remembering the thrill that

had soared through her when Alex had pulled the
ring from his shirt pocket and presented it to her.
The shy, almost embarrassed way he'd slipped it on
her finger.

Paige had kissed him then, so full of passion for
him that it had scorched her down to her very soul.
Alex had lost all of his shyness, pulling her tightly
against him and ravishing her lips with his mouth.
She breathed a deep, wistful sigh, remembering the
moment and the desire she could have sworn she'd
seen in his eyes.

Paige had believed that they would finally con-
summate their relationship that night...but had only
been disappointed once again.

Alex had wanted to wait until their wedding
night. Had murmured something about wanting to
make it special between them. She'd actually
thought it rather sweet at the time—as well as a little
frustrating.

Now she knew it had been a sign.

A bad sign. Alex hadn't wanted her after all.
Something...something about *her* had made him
change his mind. He hadn't even bothered to explain the reason in the note he'd left, which had contained only two words: *Sorry, Alex.* She'd spent
months going over every moment they'd spent together, trying to figure out what she'd done wrong.

After months of torturous soul-searching and
endless phone conversations with her friends ana-

lyzing every angle of the relationship, Paige had finally figured it out. She'd fallen in love with a jerk.

A handsome, sexy, charming jerk, but a jerk all the same. Paige blamed herself for indulging in a whirlwind romance. For agreeing to marry a man she'd known for barely a month. For letting him break her heart.

She blamed Alex for everything else. The cowardly way he ran off before the wedding. All the silly UFO hype that had followed. But most of all, she blamed him for the way he'd made her doubt herself.

So it was time to put him in the past once and for all. After tonight she'd never think about or cry over Alex again. Maybe her mother would even follow her example, though Paige didn't hold out much hope.

Margo Weaver didn't handle loss well. She'd had a mental breakdown twelve years ago when Paige's father had been killed in a car accident, refusing to accept his death. Just like she was refusing to accept the fact that her second husband wasn't coming back. Margo was certain Stanley would return to her some day—as soon as the aliens let him go.

Paige didn't want to end up like her mother—clinging to a crazy fantasy instead of accepting reality. Carefully pulling the chain over her head, she undid the clasp and the diamond ring fell into her palm. The platinum band glistened in the waning sunlight. She closed her fist around it, then hurled it over the balcony. "Goodbye, Alex."

She leaned over the railing to watch the ring fly through the air. It bounced down the sidewalk several feet before she finally lost sight of it.

Gone forever. Just like Alex.

A perfect ending to what she'd once believed was a perfect love.

Paige straightened and turned, her heart lighter than it had been for a long time. She walked over to the table, blew out the candles, then dumped the éclairs into the trash. She intended to leave all the rest behind—the dishes, the candlesticks, the champagne. A thank-you to Franco for lending her the skirt for the evening. She had no reason to ever return to this apartment.

Paige opened the door, ready to step into her new life.

And saw Alex Mack standing on the other side.

She grabbed the doorjamb to keep from falling over, his sexy smile still able to make her heart bounce in her chest.

Then he said, "Hi, honey. I'm home."

2

ALEX KNEW he'd said the wrong thing as soon as the words came tumbling out of his mouth. His communication skills had obviously suffered from lack of exercise in the last year. That's what happened when you found yourself confined to a ten-by-ten cell twenty hours out of every day for twelve straight months.

He was lucky he could speak at all with Paige standing there in front of him after all this time. A Paige he almost didn't recognize.

She'd cut her beautiful long hair. Ditched her classic conservative clothes for a red halter top and a short black skirt that made him stare at her legs for far too long. Then his gaze fell lower and he saw the fire-red polish on her toenails. He blinked and looked down toward her feet again. Was that a tattoo on her ankle?

His gaze moved slowly up her lush body as his tongue struggled for something intelligent to say. She looked incredible. He'd dreamed of this moment every day for the past year. Dreamed of her. Now he stood here gaping at her like an idiot, wanting to tell her how much he'd missed her. How much he wanted to hold her again and never let her go.

But before he could say a word, Paige made her own feelings perfectly clear. She slammed the door in his face.

Alex stood staring at the solid oak in shocked disbelief. The old Paige would have given him a chance to explain. She would have listened quietly to his side of the story and tried to understand. This new Paige, judging by the homicidal sparks he'd just seen in her big blue eyes, wasn't interested in his explanation.

Tough.

Alex put up his fist and pounded hard on the door. He hadn't come this far—or given up this much—to turn back now. "Paige, let me in."

"Go away!"

"We need to talk."

"You're three hundred and sixty-five days too late!"

He reached for the knob. "Open this door."

"I'm warning you, Alex," she shouted from the other side. "If you don't leave right now, I'm calling the police."

"I'm not going anywhere." Alex wiggled the doorknob but it stayed firmly locked. "And I'm warning you. If you don't open this door by the time I count to three, I'm going to knock it down."

Silence. The door didn't budge.

"One." he called out, certain she'd open it before he got to three. Paige was a reasonable person. She wouldn't call his bluff.

"Two." Then again, he hadn't seen her for a year. Maybe she'd changed on the inside as well as on the outside. He backed up a step, trying to gauge the thickness of the wood. He'd never actually knocked a door down before, though it always seemed easy enough in the movies. He backed up another couple of steps.

"Three!"

Alex lowered his shoulder and barreled forward at the same moment the door swung open. Paige sidestepped out of his way to avoid a collision. Alex wasn't quite so lucky. He flew inside the room and careened into a table. The dishes and candlesticks on it went flying, crashing onto the floor. Like Alex.

For a moment he just lay there, trying to remain conscious after banging the back of his head on a chair. Shards of china and glass surrounded him. Something wet seeped through the back of his shirt.

At last he looked up to see Paige gazing down at him. "Guess you called my bluff."

"Now it looks like I should call an ambulance."

He shifted on the floor, wincing slightly at a sharp pain in his right shoulder. "You're not getting rid of me so easily."

She planted her hands on her hips. "So what do I have to do to get you to leave? Set another wedding date?"

"Look, Paige..." Alex got up on one knee, then grew so dizzy he had to grab the leg of an overturned chair.

Paige reached out one hand to steady his shoulder. "Are you all right?"

Was that concern he heard in her voice? It gave him hope and enough encouragement to rise unsteadily to his feet. "I think so."

"Too bad."

So much for her concern. The momentary dizziness passed and he wiped his hand across the sticky wetness on the back of his shirt. "What's this?"

"Champagne. Dom Pérignon, 1992. A very good year."

Too late Alex realized that Paige must be expecting someone. He'd glimpsed the intimate table setting for two just before he'd crashed into it. The candles. The champagne. Hell.

She was expecting a man.

Jealousy washed over him like a tidal wave. Just the thought of another man touching Paige made him want to grab her in his arms and stake his claim. Alex took a deep breath, then another, a little stunned by his visceral reaction to the fact that she was dating. Had he really expected her to wait for him? Especially when he'd given her no indication that he was coming back?

Yes.

His faith in Paige's love had made it possible to endure the hell of the last year. He'd assumed she'd be angry. Hurt. Confused. But he'd never even considered the possibility that she'd move on to another man.

Which proved that he truly was an idiot. She was gorgeous. Then again, she'd always been beautiful to him. But now she was different. The shy, reserved Paige of his memory was gone. The woman before him now was full of fire. A kitten who had morphed into a hellcat.

But she was *his* hellcat. Alex would make that fact perfectly clear to any man who happened to walk through the door.

Paige took a step toward him, her brow furrowed. "You're bleeding."

He followed her gaze to the front of his gray T-shirt and saw a small red stain spreading in a circle on his chest. No doubt he'd landed on one of the slivers of glass on the floor.

"Don't get your hopes up," he said wryly. "It's probably not serious."

She met his gaze. "You might need stitches."

Pulling his T-shirt over his head, he wadded it up into a ball then dabbed away the blood on his chest. "See? Nothing serious. You can barely see the cut."

She wrenched her gaze up from his chest and cleared her throat, her cheeks flushed. "Good. Okay, well, you can leave now."

He tossed the shirt aside. "You're awfully eager to get rid of me. Afraid your date won't like finding another man here alone with you?"

She blinked. "My what?" Then her eyes narrowed. "Wait a minute, how did you know where to find me?"

"This is where you live," he replied, confused by her question. He probably had a concussion.

She shook her head. "Not anymore. I sold this apartment eleven months ago."

Alex couldn't believe it. She had fallen in love with this old place the moment she'd set eyes on it. He remembered the way she'd danced around the apartment when she'd given him a tour after making the down payment, almost giddy with excitement. The way she'd wanted to turn it into the perfect newlywed nest—a place for just the two of them.

But most of all, he remembered the hot kiss she'd given him on the balcony. The lushness of her body pressed into his own. Her soft whispers of love in his ear.

He sucked in a deep breath, the ache of those memories slicing deeper than the superficial cut on his chest. He'd been fooling himself that they'd be able to resume where they'd left off after he explained everything.

Well, not *everything.*

He planned to tell her just enough to make her understand. Enough to keep her from asking more questions—questions he couldn't answer. But now he sensed it wasn't going to be that easy.

That didn't stop him from asking a question of his

own. "If you sold the apartment, why are you here now?"

"That's really none of your business."

Jealousy flared up in him once more. Was she living with another man? He looked around the room. "This doesn't look like your furniture."

"You're right, it's not," she replied, with no further explanation.

"So what is it doing here? What are *you* doing here, Paige?"

She picked up one of the chairs and set it upright on the floor. "If you must know, I'm leasing the place on a time-share basis—weekends only. I thought it would give me a chance to get away from everything."

That did make sense. He'd met her mother. But his instincts told him there was still something she wasn't telling him. A year ago, Alex would have pushed her for a clearer answer. Digging deeper. Always digging. Paige had mentioned once that she liked the way he always listened to her. She hadn't realized that was his job.

Paige's voice cut through his reverie. "So why are *you* here?"

"Because I want to explain why I left."

"Don't bother. There's absolutely nothing you can say that will change anything."

"Maybe not. But I'll feel better."

She arched a finely winged brow. "This may

come as a shock, Alex, but making you feel better isn't high on my list of priorities."

She was bitter. He couldn't blame her. But Paige deserved to know the truth. *Needed* to know the truth. At least, some of it.

"I didn't mean to hurt you," he blurted, realizing too late he should have rehearsed what he was going to say to her. He'd certainly had long enough to do it. "Everything just got out of control."

"You should have told me you were having second thoughts," she said haltingly. "Instead, you just...left."

"Under the circumstances, I thought that would be for the best."

"Best for you, maybe. You didn't have to announce to everybody that the wedding was off. You didn't have to deal with the caterer or the reception hall or the band. You didn't have to pretend your heart wasn't broken...." She sucked in a deep breath, then tipped up her chin. "Don't you see, Alex? You did more than dump me. You humiliated me."

Her words hit him low in the gut. Wrenching. Twisting. He braced himself against the pain, knowing it was only going to get worse before the night was over. He glanced at the door, tempted to walk out. To let her think he'd just suffered a case of cold feet.

But that wasn't the case. He'd waited a year for

this moment. Marking off every day on the calendar until he could tell her what was in his heart.

Alex didn't plan to waste another second. "I'm sorry about everything you went through, Paige. But I have to make one thing perfectly clear."

"What?" she asked.

"I never asked you to marry me."

PAIGE STARED AT HIM, wondering if the collision with the floor had affected his brain. "That's not true. I still have the proposal you e-mailed me." She looked at the gray ashes scattered on the messy floor. "At least I had it until a few minutes ago."

"I agree you received a proposal," Alex said slowly, "but it wasn't from me."

Paige reached blindly behind her for a chair and sat down. Maybe it was the champagne or the shock of seeing Alex again or the fact that he wasn't wearing a shirt, but for some reason her knees felt a little wobbly.

"Are you just trying to torture me?" she asked. "I'm finally over you, Alex. The last thing I need is for you to come barging back into my life, causing more chaos. So I suggest you leave. Now. For both our sakes."

A muscle flexed in his jaw. "Just hear me out first."

Nobody could say she hadn't warned him. "Okay, fine. Tell your story."

Alex pulled up another chair beside her, straddling the back of it in one easy motion. She couldn't help but notice the ripple of taut muscle over his chest and belly. He was slimmer than he'd been a year ago. Fitter. Maybe the time away from her had been good for him. Maybe Franco had a shirt he could borrow.

When Paige met his gaze again, she couldn't help but feel that Alex was a virtual stranger. Those wonderful few weeks of their whirlwind courtship almost seemed like a blur now. A crazy dream. Had she really agreed to marry this man?

"Promise me you'll hear me out," Alex said. "No matter what I say, you won't leave or try to kick me out until I'm done."

Her stomach twisted. It must really be bad. Was there another woman? Was he married? Was he an alien? Paige shook those unsettling thoughts from her head. She'd been spending too much time with her mother. "Okay, I promise."

He hesitated, as if not sure how to begin. "Our first meeting was a setup, Paige. I was supposed to bump into you that day on the wharf. I was supposed to make you fall in love with me."

Her mind flashed back to that fateful day on Fisherman's Wharf, a place she loved despite all the tourist trappings. She spent almost every Sunday there if the weather was decent. It had been sunny the day she'd met Alex, if a little cool. She'd worn a khaki jacket. Alex had spilled raspberry iced tea on it when he'd bumped into her.

Now he was here telling her that had all been staged. All part of some scheme. Which left her with one simple question. "Why?"

"Because I was assigned to find information about your missing stepfather. We didn't buy the story about his abduction by a UFO. We thought you and your mother were hiding the truth. So if I got close to you..."

"You could find out what really happened," Paige breathed. It was all starting to make horrible sense to her now. The police had been called after her stepfather's disappearance but they'd been highly skeptical of Margo's UFO explanation. Even speculating that her mother might have something do with Stanley's disappearance.

They'd obviously decided to send in one of their own to determine if there had been foul play. And what better way to get to the mother than through the daughter?

It also explained why Alex had never shared much about himself or his family. The fact that she'd never been to his home—or even knew his address. The way he'd listen so patiently when she talked on and on. The fact that he never complained about spending time with her kooky mother. She'd watched enough shows about undercover cops to know that's how they operated.

No wonder she'd thought of him as a stranger just now. He was a stranger. And she'd been ready to marry him!

The impact of her own stupidity made her slump back in her chair. Alex had just been doing his job. He'd never cared about her. Never loved her. Never even been attracted to her.

Her cheeks flamed when she thought about the reason he'd given her for not wanting to make love. How he'd wanted to wait until their wedding night. She'd thought him an old-fashioned romantic at the time. *What a fool.*

One tiny, rational part of her brain told her she'd be even more upset if he'd slept with her under false pretenses, but Paige was in no mood to be rational.

"I think you'd better leave," she said with an odd calmness she was far from feeling.

"I'm not done."

She looked at him in disbelief. "There's more?"

He gave a brisk nod. "I never meant our relationship to go that far. The engagement, I mean. That e-mail proposal was sent by someone else. Someone who thought an engagement between us might make you open up to me."

She was going to be sick. Or else she was going to shoot him. The latter sounded more enjoyable than the former. If only she had a gun...and knew how to operate one. Maybe Alex would give her a few lessons. It was the least he could do after lying to her.

"I meant to call off the wedding before it was too late, Paige," he continued. "But everything just spun out of control. I'm sorry."

He was sorry. As if that made everything all right.

Alex sat there shirtless in front of her, patiently letting her absorb everything in silence. Looking so
sexy that she wanted to scream. It wasn't fair. She'd
been wild about him and he'd been...faking it.

She met his gaze and the expression on her face
made him scoot his chair back a notch.

"Are you done?" she asked.

"For now." He leaned forward. "I know this isn't
easy to hear, Paige, but I thought you deserved to
know the truth."

In her opinion, truth was highly overrated. She
would have preferred to keep believing he'd
dumped her, just like every other man in her life.

It was pathetic, really. During the past year, Paige
had come to the depressing realization that every
relationship she'd ever had, beginning when she
was fifteen years old, had been ended by her male
counterpart. Not once had she been the dumper instead of the dumpee. Not once had *she* broken someone's heart.

She wouldn't mind breaking Alex's heart right
now. Along with other assorted appendages. Most
of which she'd never seen before. She wasn't sure
which was worse. The fact that he'd been playing
her or that it had been so easy for him to do.

Talk about insulting. She mentally cringed at the
thought of that night on the balcony. She'd brought
him here to show him the apartment, blabbering
endlessly about their future life together. Then

she'd kissed him, practically throwing herself at him. But he'd nobly resisted her advances.

Saint Alex.

Now he was back, confessing all, looking for redemption. Fat chance. She'd rather push him off the balcony.

"Are you all right?" he asked at last, his face searching her own.

"It's a little stuffy in here." She fanned her warm cheeks, then looked toward the open balcony doors. "I could use some fresh air."

The door chime forestalled his reply. Paige set her jaw and walked to the door, opening it to reveal two uniformed policemen.

"Please come in, officers."

Alex slowly stood up as the cops entered the apartment, his gaze wary. "What's going on?"

The older cop took in the shattered dishes on the floor and the upturned table. "That's what we want to know. We received a telephone call from this apartment about a possible domestic disturbance."

Alex turned to her. "You called the police?"

She nodded. "Just like I warned you I was going to do. Unlike you, Alex, I mean what I say."

He took a step towards her but the younger cop moved into his path, putting himself squarely between Alex and Paige.

"Listen to me, Paige," Alex entreated, craning his neck around the officer. "Despite everything, I fell in love with you. I've never stopped loving you."

The older cop turned to her. "Are you all right, ma'am?"

"I'm not sure," Paige said honestly.

"Look," Alex explained, turning to the cops, "the two of us just need some time alone to work things out."

"That's what they all say," the younger cop muttered under his breath.

The older cop ushered Paige to a chair. "Would you like to file a complaint?"

"What happens if I do?" she asked.

"We'll take this man with us and make sure he doesn't bother you again."

"You mean arrest him?"

The cop nodded. "If you're willing to file charges."

She looked at Alex. "Absolutely."

"Paige, this is crazy!" Alex exclaimed as the younger cop pulled out a pair of handcuffs. "Tell them there's been a mistake. Explain what really happened."

"All right." She turned to the cops. "Mr. Mack threatened to break down my door, then he barged in here and broke all of my good dishes. Then he proceeded to take his shirt off. Is that enough to file charges?"

The younger cop nodded. "Trespassing. Destruction of private property. Attempted assault. What do you think, Bill?"

"Sounds like he wins a trip down to the county jail to me. All expenses paid."

Alex didn't struggle as they led him out of the apartment in handcuffs. He just stared at Paige in stunned disbelief until they'd crossed the threshold and disappeared down the long hallway.

Paige followed after them. "Wait a minute, officers."

The younger cop turned to her at the top of the stairs. "Yes, ma'am?"

Hope lit Alex's dark eyes. The same eyes that had haunted her dreams for the last year.

"He forgot his shirt." She shove the wadded gray T-shirt between Alex's cuffed wrists, then turned back into the apartment and shut the door.

It wasn't a gun or a shove off the balcony, but it was enough.

For now.

3

MY LATEST SUBJECT is Paige Hanover. She's young and cute, the perfect prototype to test the power of the skirt. I'm thinking Ashley Judd to play her in the movie. Naturally, I didn't tell her I'm writing a screenplay about the skirt's effect on men. Things definitely sounded interesting upstairs after that young Greek stud headed up to her apartment. Lots of shouting and the sound of dishes breaking.

Did the sight of Paige in that skirt make the man go berserk? I know the aphrodisiac effect of the unique fabric is said to be quite powerful. However, it appears Paige wasn't open to his advances. I saw the police take her hot-blooded admirer away in handcuffs. Perhaps I could make my screenplay a murder mystery. I'll have to see what develops from here....

TWO DAYS LATER, Paige sat at her desk in the back office of Bay Bouquets. She'd inherited the business after her father's death in a traffic accident had left her as Grandpa Hanover's only heir. Her grandfather had taken Paige and her mother in shortly after Margo's breakdown, giving her mother a job as a clerk in the store after she'd recovered while making Paige his apprentice. Grandpa Hanover had not only given Paige full ownership of Bay Bouquets in his will five years ago, but left her his house as well.

She'd inherited his natural talent with flowers, but not with numbers. She bent over the desk, trying to concentrate on the invoices and accounts receivable in front of her. There were some days she just wanted to chuck it all and camp out on a mountaintop somewhere and stare at the stars.

But that would meaning selling the store and Paige couldn't conceive of letting go of her grandfather's legacy. It had meant too much to him. Besides, her mother worked here, too, as well as Lena, a longtime assistant who could practically run the place by herself.

"More fan mail." Her mother walked into the office and dropped a bundle of envelopes on top of the desk. Margo Weaver was half a foot shorter than her daughter, with ash-blonde hair, bright green eyes and a button nose. She wore a pink knit warmup suit today with matching pink tennis shoes.

"I don't want to read them," Paige replied.

"But these are all addressed to you." Margo pulled a chair up beside the desk and sat down with a contented sigh. "*UFO Watch* aired that segment about Alex's disappearance again Saturday night."

"I know," she said with a groan. "I saw it."

Then she'd seen Alex. Literally. Although she hadn't told her mother about their meeting—or about having him arrested.

She'd had two days to cool off and now Paige wondered if she might have overreacted just a little. Yes, Alex had taken her by surprise. Yes, she'd been stunned to learn that he'd romanced her under false pretenses.

Stunned might be an understatement. Paige was still reeling. She was also hurt and disillusioned. But as much as she wanted to wreak some old-fashioned justice, nothing that Alex had done to her was actually criminal.

Infuriating, but unfortunately not illegal.

Which left her with two alternatives. She could pursue revenge through the court system and let the lawyers worry about all the legalities. Or she could drop the charges and forget about her ex-fiancé once and for all. The former was the most tempting, but it also meant putting Alex front and center in her life once again.

"Earth to Paige."

She looked up to see her mother's forehead crinkled in concern.

"What's wrong?" Margo asked.

"Nothing." Paige stared blankly at the order forms on her desk.

"You're thinking about Alex," Margo surmised. "I can always tell. You get this look on your face."

That settled it. "Alex is history."

Margo reached across the desk and patted her daughter's hand. "I know how you feel. Some days I worry that Stanley is never coming back."

"Maybe it's time to file for divorce," Paige suggested for the hundredth time since Stanley had left her mother. "Time to move on with your life."

Margo shook her head. "I can't give up hope. Not when there's a chance Stanley may return to me. I know you think it's silly to give interviews to shows like *UFO Watch*, but maybe someone will be watching who can help us find Stanley and Alex."

"Have you read any of these letters, Mom?" Paige pointed to the stack on her desk. "They're all from crackpots."

Margo sniffed. "Just because you don't happen to believe in the existence of UFOs or alien abductions doesn't make the rest of us crackpots."

Paige swallowed her retort. They'd had this argument before and it had never gotten them anywhere. Margo clung tenaciously to the belief that her husband had left her against his will. Abduction by aliens seemed preferable to the possibility that he had simply walked away.

"How long are you going to wait for Stanley to come back to you, Mom?" Paige asked softly. "Another year? Five years? Ten?"

The chime of the laser door alarm signaled a customer had walked into the shop. Margo headed out of the office, pausing only a moment to reply to her daughter. "I'll wait for him just as long as it takes, Paige. We shouldn't give up on the people we love."

Paige shook her head as her mother disappeared from the doorway. In her opinion, there was a huge difference between giving up and clinging to a romantic delusion. She'd waited a full year for the man she loved to come back to her. A man she now knew had never loved her at all. She didn't intend to waste one more minute on Alex Mack.

Picking up the telephone, she looked up the number of the local precinct in the directory, then dialed the police. It took three operator transfers before she finally reached someone who could help her.

"Sergeant Phelps," barked a low voice on the other end of the line.

"Hello, this is Paige Hanover. I filed a complaint against Alex Mack on Saturday night and the police took him to jail. But now I'm thinking about dropping the charges."

"Will you spell his last name for me, please."

"It's Mack—*M-A-C-K*."

"Hold on," he said in a clipped voice. She could hear voices in the background, as well as the shuffle of papers and the rapid-fire click of computer keys.

"Yes, we've got an Alex Mack in custody," the sergeant said a few moments later. "He just posted bail. Alex Mack aka Alexander Mackopoulos."

"Alexander who?" Paige couldn't have heard him right.

"Alex Mack is an alias," the sergeant informed him. "His legal name is Alexander Mackopoulos."

Her grip tightened on the phone. "Are you absolutely certain we're talking about the same man?"

"I'm positive. Alexander Mackopoulos was brought in this past Saturday night on charges of trespassing, destruction of private property and attempted assault."

"Those were the charges," Paige concurred, "but are you sure about the name?"

"It's the same name that was on file when he was released from county jail a week ago," Sergeant Phelps replied. "The fingerprints are the same, too."

"Did you say county jail?"

His tone grew impatient. "Do you have a hearing problem, ma'am?"

"Why was Alex in jail?"

"We're not allowed to release that information over the telephone. If you plan to drop the charges against him, then you'll need to come down to the station and fill out the paperwork."

"I will. Thank you, Sergeant." Her head whirled as she hung up the phone. Alex Mack wasn't Alex Mack. He was Alexander Mackopoulos. Ex-fiancé and ex-convict.

A complete stranger. She hadn't even known the real name of the man she'd been about to marry. When Alex had shown up Saturday night and confessed that he'd been assigned to romance her, she'd just assumed he was a cop. A silly assumption, now that she thought about it. Would the police have arrested one of their own so easily? The officers who had taken him away in handcuffs Saturday night certainly hadn't seemed to recognize him.

So if Alex wasn't a cop, why had he been looking for her stepfather? Why had he been in jail? And why had he suddenly popped back into her life after all this time?

And the most important question of all—what was Paige going to do now?

LATE MONDAY MORNING, Alex walked out of the San Francisco county jail a free man. Temporarily, anyway.

His older half brother, Nico, waited for him in the narrow hallway, one burly shoulder propped against the painted cinder block. "I think we need to have a talk."

"I don't want to hear it," Alex said, walking past him. Nico had always had an annoying habit of trying to tell him what to do. It had gotten even worse after their father died three months ago, when Nico had declared himself the head of the Mackopoulos family.

But his brother didn't give up easily. "I just shelled out five hundred dollars, so I think you can listen to what I have to say."

Listening to Nico was what had gotten him into this mess with Paige in the first place. "Don't worry, I'll pay you back every penny."

Five hundred dollars had been the price of his bond, set by the judge less than an hour ago. His court date was scheduled for one month from today.

"I don't give a damn about the money," Nico said as they walked out of the courthouse and into bright California sunshine. "But I am worried about our mother getting wind of this. She's been through enough lately."

Alex couldn't argue with that. The death of Lucian Mackopoulos had hit his wife Thea very hard. It amazed Alex that she could love that old man so much. Enough to forgive him for cheating on her twenty-nine years ago.

Enough to take his bastard son into her home.

Thea had always treated Alex as one of her own. She'd loved him unconditionally, even though he must have been a daily reminder of her husband's infidelity. She'd never made him feel like an interloper in the Mackopoulos home, expecting everyone to treat him like a member of the family or face her wrath.

Not that his stepmother was the least bit intimidating. She was warm and loving, with a talent for cooking that had earned her a reputation for serving some of the best Greek cuisine in San Francisco. She'd toyed with the idea of opening a restaurant, but she had never followed through, insisting that her family came first. That was only one of the reasons Alex would protect her with his life. And why he'd gone to jail for her.

"Just explain to me why you'd be crazy enough to pay a visit to Paige Hanover after all this time?" Nico dug in his pocket for his car keys.

Alex stopped next to the vintage red Corvette that belonged to his brother. "None of your damn business."

"If it affects this family, then it is my business." Nico pushed the unlock button on his remote control, then popped open the door. "What exactly did you tell her, Alex?"

"Enough to get me thrown into jail." Alex slid into the front passenger seat, then unspooled the seat belt. He was in no mood to deal with his overbearing brother today.

"Do you know what your problem is?" Nico asked.

Alex clenched his jaw. "I'm sure you'll be happy to tell me."

"You're too damn noble. You probably went to see her so you could apologize. Am I right?"

"You think you are. That's all that ever matters."

Nico gripped the steering wheel of the parked car as he stared straight ahead. "Just tell me you didn't spill all the family secrets to clear your conscience."

Alex turned to look at him. "I went to jail for almost a year to keep our father's secret. A Mackopoulos never breaks his word."

"Then promise me you won't see her again."

Alex stared out the passenger window. "I can't do that."

"Why not?"

He couldn't tell Nico the real reason. That Paige had gotten under his skin a year ago and no matter how hard he tried, he couldn't seem to forget her. Need for her pulsed through his veins, even after she'd had him thrown in jail. But Alex wasn't about to give up. A Mackopoulos never surrendered.

Unfortunately, his brother shared that same trait. Which made it difficult to deal with him whenever they disagreed. Like now, for instance.

"Just drop me off at Bay Bouquets in the Embarcadero Center. We'll talk about this later."

Nico narrowed his eyes. "Paige's flower shop? Are you crazy? She had you locked up the last time you saw her. She might shoot you this time."

"She's not a violent person," Alex said, hoping it was true. He'd never seen Paige as angry as she'd been the other night, her cheeks flushed with indignation and her blue eyes flashing fire. But passion burned underneath that fire. He could see it in the way she looked at him.

"How much does she know?" Nico asked, pulling out of the parking lot.

Alex turned to him. "She knows I dated her to try and gather information about her stepfather. She doesn't know why. Or that you were the one who sent her that damn e-mail proposal."

"I only sent it because you weren't making any

progress in locating Stanley Weaver. It's obvious to me now that I should have done the job myself."

The thought of Nico romancing Paige set Alex's teeth on edge. "She couldn't have told you what she didn't know."

"Maybe," Nico conceded. "But it looks like I'll be making her acquaintance anyway."

Alex frowned at him. "Why?"

"To convince her to drop these ridiculous charges against you. I don't want you spending another minute in jail. Not when I should have gone in your place."

He was talking about the year Alex had been incarcerated on contempt charges for refusing to testify before a grand jury. It had been his bad luck to draw a hardnosed judge who routinely jailed witnesses until they agreed to talk. A judge who didn't care that Lucian Mackopoulos, the owner of the company under investigation for illegal distribution of funds, was too ill to even realize what was happening.

Alex thought back to how it had all started, when Nico had come across a blackmail threat meant for their father. There was an audiotape, proving that Lucian had recently had a fling with a stripper in his private office, along with a threat promising to send the tape to Thea unless their father handed over twenty thousand dollars.

The blackmailer obviously didn't know that Lucian had just suffered his first heart attack the day before. Nico, shocked by the evidence of his father's betrayal, had paid the money to protect his mother. That had been his first mistake. His second had been withdrawing the funds from the company account.

By the time he'd confided in Alex, it had been too late. An overzealous IRS agent had caught the discrepancy months later and an investigation had begun.

Alex and Nico had begun an investigation of their own during that time, after the security firm they'd hired had pegged Stanley Weaver as the probable blackmailer. That's when Alex had gone undercover as Paige's boyfriend, hoping to discover Stanley's whereabouts and try to find the original of the explosive audiotape.

But nothing had turned out as they'd planned. And neither Alex nor Nico could reveal the truth behind the missing twenty thousand dollars. Not without breaking their mother's heart.

If Lucian hadn't died of heart complications three months ago, Alex might still be in jail. They'd let him out just long enough to tell his father goodbye. Just long enough for Lucian to extract a promise from both his sons to take good care of their mother.

A promise they both intended to keep.

With Lucian's death, the investigation against Mackopoulos Imports came to a grinding halt. But it still took almost twelve weeks before the case was officially closed and Alex was released from jail. He certainly didn't intend to go back again.

"I'll talk to Paige myself," Alex said.

"Are you sure?" Nico asked him, turning into the Embarcadero Center. "I'll be happy to handle it for you."

"I'm sure," he said firmly.

Alex tried to ignore the thrill of anticipation in the pit of his stomach. He hadn't been able to stop thinking about her all weekend. Despite the fact that she'd had him thrown in jail, he still wanted her.

In truth, he wanted her more now than when he'd been forced to leave her a year ago. But he still couldn't tell her about the grand-jury proceedings. Or the contempt charges. Not without revealing everything.

Alex rubbed one hand over his face, realizing Paige would probably never let him near her again. But at least now he had an excuse. A reason to see her again. It was a step in the right direction.

Nico pulled up to the curb in front of Bay Bouquets. "Just let me know if she gives you any more trouble."

"Thanks for the ride," Alex said, climbing out of the Corvette. He didn't want Nico within one hundred feet of Paige. The intensity of his possessiveness shocked him. It also made one thing perfectly clear.

He wanted Paige back. For real this time.

Alex walked into the shop as the Corvette spun away. The scent of roses hit him immediately and he remembered the day he'd come to pick her up here for their first date. He'd intended to approach the project without emotion, just like he approached his job as the financial manager for his father's company. But those intentions had evaporated the first time Paige had smiled at him.

And he'd never recovered.

When Alex walked inside the shop, his arrival set off a door chime and he saw Paige's mother, Margo Weaver, turn from the potted rosebush she was grooming to greet him.

But the moment she saw his face, she fell to the floor in a dead faint.

Alex rushed around the counter, kneeling down beside her. He picked up the pruning shears that lay partially beneath her, then softly called her name. "Margo?"

The sound of footsteps made him look up. He saw Paige gaping at him, horror in her big blue eyes as she looked at her unconscious mother on the floor, then at the pruning shears he still held in his hand.

"Get away from my mother!"

4

PAIGE CHARGED toward Alex as he straightened to his full height. Her heart raced in her chest, but she couldn't completely blame that reaction on fear.

"What did you do to her?"

"Nothing," he exclaimed, holding his hands out helplessly. "I just walked through the front door. She took one look at me and hit the floor."

Paige moved to place herself between him and Margo. "Then why are you holding those?"

Alex looked down at the pruning shears in his right hand as if he'd never seen them before. "They fell out of your mother's hand when she fainted. I thought it might be dangerous to leave them on the floor in case she started to flop around or something."

Paige knelt down beside her mother, telling herself not to trust him. Despite falling madly in love with Alex a year ago, she didn't know anything about him. A fact that still nagged at her.

Margo moaned and Paige sensed Alex moving closer beside her. Her traitorous body reacted to his

nearness, a strange tingling emanating from somewhere deep inside of her.

"Is she all right?" he asked in a low voice.
"Should I call an ambulance?"

"No," Paige replied, picking up her mother's
limp hand from the floor and rubbing it vigorously
between her own. "She's fainted before. It's how she
reacts to a shock."

The last time had been the night her husband disappeared. Margo had taken Paige out into the backyard to show her the unusual burn marks in the
lawn. While they were outside, her mother had
come across Stanley's pocket watch half-hidden in
the grass, the one she'd given him on their wedding
day. And she'd fainted dead away.

"You didn't tell her I was back?" Alex asked. "Or
why I left?"

Paige remembered her own shock at seeing him
at the door of the apartment. "No. And I'd appreciate it if you didn't tell her, either. It's bad enough
everyone thinks you didn't want to marry me. I'd
prefer they didn't learn you didn't even want to
date me."

"That's not true...." Alex protested, but another
moan from Margo cut him off.

Paige kept rubbing her hand and soon Margo's
eyelids began to flutter.

"Mom?"

Margo opened her eyes and looked up at her
daughter. "What...happened?"

"You fainted," Paige replied, relieved to see some color flow back into her mother's cheeks.

Margo's gaze moved over her shoulder to where Alex stood. Her eyes widened. "He's back."

Paige reached for a large green florist's sponge on the shelf behind her, then pillowed it gently beneath her mother's head. "I know."

Margo stared up at her daughter. "But how can you be so calm about this? It's a miracle!"

"Not quite," Paige said, reaching for her mother's other hand. "Let's try to sit you up."

Margo shook off her help, then rose gingerly to her knees. "I'm fine. I just can't believe they let Alex go."

"They?" Alex intoned as Paige stifled a groan.

"The aliens who abducted you," Margo explained. She grabbed the edge of the counter and hauled herself to her feet. "Just like my poor Stanley."

Alex skittered a glance toward Paige and she knew he was about to suggest calling an ambulance again.

"Mom's still a UFO buff," she explained, brushing the floor dust off the back of her mother's blue jumper. "She believes anyone who disappears under mysterious circumstances was the victim of alien foul play."

"Not just anyone," Margo countered. "But when there's no other reasonable explanation, it has to be considered." Then she turned to Alex. "So is there?"

"Is there what?"

"A reasonable explanation for why you left my daughter at the altar a year ago? Why you broke her heart?"

Alex met Paige's gaze and after a long silent moment said, "No."

Paige didn't know if he was simply acceding to her wish not to reveal the real reason or if his answer meant something more. Then she mentally kicked herself for playing into her fantasies about him again.

She'd done enough of that a year ago. Believing that Alex, a man she'd known only a few short weeks, had fallen madly in love with her, Paige had found a way to rationalize anything that didn't make sense in their relationship. His e-mail marriage proposal. His reticence to talk about family or friends. His reluctance to sleep with her.

Just like her mother rationalized Stanley's abandonment by claiming he was abducted by a UFO. A coping mechanism that had kept her mother from moving forward for almost two years. Paige wasn't about to fall into the same trap. She wanted to live in the real world, no matter how painful or unpleasant it might be.

"Maybe you'd better go lay down in the back room for a while," Paige suggested to her mother.

"Nonsense," Margo replied. "I'm fine." Then she looked around the shop. "Where's Mr. Rooney?"

"Who?"

"Mr. Rooney." Margo frowned. "I was talking with him right before Alex walked in. He was standing over there, by the bougainvillea display."

All three of them looked at the corner of the empty shop. Then Paige turned to Alex. "Did you see him when you came in? Or see anyone leave?"

When Alex shook his head, Paige turned to her mother. "Are you sure you're all right? Maybe you hit your head when you fainted?"

"Mr. Rooney is not a figment of my imagination," Margo replied, bring her fingertips up to rub her temple. "He's about my age. Gray hair. Neatly trimmed mustache. Quite handsome. He was in here. I know it!"

Paige didn't say anything, fearing for her mother's mental health. It was bad enough her mother believed in UFOs. Was she now seeing imaginary men?

Margo cleared her throat. "Maybe I will go lie down for a little while, if you don't mind handling the store all by yourself."

"I'll keep Paige company," Alex announced.

"That's not necessary," Paige muttered under her breath.

"It will be my pleasure."

Margo reached out and touched his arm, as if to assure herself Alex was real. "Will I see you again?"

"I hope so," he replied, placing his big hand gently over hers. "But that's up to Paige."

She watched her mother melt under the heat of

Alex's smile. Just as she'd done herself too many times in the past. He had used that smile when he'd wanted to distract her from something. Like questions she'd asked that he didn't want to answer. Questions about his family or his past. Anything that might have given her a glimpse of the real man underneath the facade.

After her mother had disappeared into the back room, Paige whirled on Alex. "I asked you not to tell her that you dated me under false pretenses last year. That doesn't mean I want her to believe we still have a future together."

He moved a step closer to her. "But what if we do?"

She blinked. "I can't believe you're doing it again. Don't worry, Alex. I've already decided to drop the charges against you, so you don't have to pretend to care about me anymore."

"Paige," he began, but she held up one hand to stop him in his tracks.

"Forget it. Forget everything that ever happened between us. In fact, I think that's the perfect reason to give my mother for your disappearance. Amnesia. I'll tell her you got hit in the head and couldn't remember anything. Not even your real name."

Her last barb didn't even make him flinch. Of course, Alex didn't realize that she knew his real name now, as well as the fact that he'd spent part of the last year in jail. Though she still didn't know why.

Other questions nagged at her, too. Why had he been so determined to find Stanley Weaver if he wasn't a cop? Why had he come back now after all this time? Just to apologize? Or did he have another motive?

Her tongue itched to ask him these questions, but she had no reason, given his track record, to believe he'd tell her the truth.

Unless she found a way to uncover it for herself.

"If you want me to tell your mother I had amnesia, I will," Alex said at last. "Frankly, I wish like hell it were true. Then maybe you'd consider giving us another chance."

"Why should I?" Paige asked at the same moment a crazy idea began flirting with her common sense.

"Because despite everything, I do care about you." He moved a step closer. "Because I haven't been able to stop thinking about you since I left. We've both changed in the last year. At least, I know I have."

Paige supposed incarceration would change a person. But for the better?

"You hate me right now," Alex continued, "which I completely understand. I hate myself for what I did to you. But I'm not here to make excuses. Or to ease my conscience. I'm here because I just can't stay away."

Paige found herself wanting to believe him. Wanting to understand what made this man tick.

But that meant playing a dangerous game. Turning the tables on Alex Mack, aka Alex Mackopoulos, and romancing him for the information that she so desperately wanted to know.

The idea gave her a certain vengeful pleasure. This time she'd be the one in control. The one who could dump *him* when it was over.

"You don't have to decide right now," he said, her long silence obviously making him uneasy. "Meet me for dinner tonight. Piccolo's at seven o'clock. You can give me your answer then."

"All right," she said, fearing he wouldn't leave until she agreed.

He smiled. "Good. I'll see you tonight, then. Seven o'clock."

"Seven o'clock," Paige echoed.

Alex looked as if he wanted to say something more, but instead he gave a brisk nod and headed out the door. When he was gone, Paige let out a breath she didn't know she'd been holding.

Piccolo's had been their favorite restaurant. The place where he'd given her the beautiful diamond engagement ring that she'd literally thrown out the window. Going there tonight would bring back a rush of memories.

Maybe that's what he was hoping for. To wear down her defenses so he could... What? Why did Alex want to rekindle a flame that had obviously never burned for him?

Paige didn't know the answer to that question. Or

to any of the other questions she knew would now keep her awake at night. Questions that would keep her from moving on with her life.

Unless she did a little investigating of her own.

ALEX'S BEDROOM in the Mackopoulos home was three times the size his jail cell had been. Yet Thea Mackopoulos was more vigilant than any jail guard could ever be.

"You're going out again?" she asked, walking into his room. "I thought we could all have dinner together tonight as a family."

"Tomorrow night," Alex promised her, standing in front of a mirror to straighten his tie.

"Here, let me do that," she offered, reaching for the clumsy knot. It had been too long since he'd dressed up in anything but an orange jumpsuit.

She fussed with his tie for a moment, then lightly patted his shirtfront. "You're too thin. You didn't eat enough in that awful jail."

"I ate as much as I could stomach."

"And I worried about you every day." She shook her head. "You're a good boy, but stubborn, like your father and your brother. I know my Lucian made some mistakes in his life, but I can't believe he did anything criminal. You should have testified. The truth would have come out."

That's exactly what Alex had feared. Protecting Thea from the truth had been the reason he'd gone to jail. The reason he and Nico had teamed up to uncover information about Paige. His stepmother believed that the investigation into her husband's finances wouldn't turn up anything. Little did she know it would break her heart.

And Alex wasn't about to tell her. His Greek father had raised his sons to revere and protect women, though Lucian Mackopoulos hadn't always practiced what he'd preached. His latest affair proved that.

So it was up to Alex and Nico to protect their mother—one of the few times they'd come together in a common cause. He just wished Paige hadn't been hurt in the process.

"So who is she?" Thea asked with a smile.

"She?"

"The woman who you find more tempting than my moussaka and *loukoumades?*"

He grinned, knowing Greek food was Thea's answer to all of life's problems. Not that he considered Paige a problem. More like a challenge. A sexy, stimulating challenge. "Her name is Paige Hanover."

Thea studied his expression. "You like her."

"Very much."

"So is this Paige Hanover the reason you've been gone for the last two nights?"

"Yes." His stepmother didn't know he'd been thrown back in jail over the weekend and Alex definitely intended to keep it that way.

"I worry about you, Alex." She reached out to

stroke his face. "Don't get me wrong, I'm thrilled that you like this girl. It's well past time for you and your brother to each find a wife. I just don't want you rushing into anything too quickly. You just got out of jail. Any woman might look good to you right now."

He grinned as he leaned over to kiss her cheek. "Don't worry, Mom, the wart on her nose and a couple of missing teeth don't bother me. It's what's inside that counts."

"Very funny." She gently swatted his arm. "Just don't let her take advantage of you."

"I think that's what Paige's mother is supposed to tell her."

"You need to hear it, too," Thea admonished. "You're a handsome man, Alex Mackopoulos. A good catch for any girl. I just question if this woman you're seeing is good enough for you. Why don't you bring her home and let me meet her. I'll know if she's the right girl for you."

Alex already knew she was the right girl—the only girl for him. But he still had to convince Paige of that fact. "You'll meet her when the time is right."

"And when will that be?" Thea challenged, folding her arms across her chest. "The day of the wedding?"

He laughed as he slipped on his jacket. "You have a lot of confidence in me, Mom. I'm not even sure Paige will want to see me again after tonight and you've already got us engaged to be married."

"That's because no woman in her right mind could turn down one of my sons." She reached out to cup his cheek. "You're both as irresistible as your father."

He heard the love in her voice for Lucian and knew once again what a remarkable woman his stepmother was. She'd forgiven her husband his transgression twenty-nine years ago. She'd even accepted his bastard son into her home. All the more reason for Alex to keep his father's last dirty secret.

"I better be going," he said, heading toward the door.

"Tell Paige that duct tape is good for warts," Thea called after him. "And that I want lots of grandchildren."

Alex wished the problem with Paige was as simple as a case of warts. But it would take more than duct tape to earn her trust again. It would take patience and understanding. Even then, there were no guarantees.

Paige had made it clear she hadn't yet forgiven him for abandoning her at the altar. That she didn't believe his reason for leaving her and didn't buy his story that he wanted her back.

But despite the odds, he had no intention of giving up. Not when her eyes told a completely different story. Alex could see the desire in those beautiful blue eyes every time she looked at him. Paige still wanted him.

She just didn't know it yet.

5

PAIGE WASN'T AN EXPERT at the revenge game, but she seemed to be adapting to it fairly well. Like not telling Alex that their favorite restaurant had been turned into an upscale gay bar. It promised to make for an interesting evening.

Her plan was simple—string Alex along until she discovered all his secrets. Then dump him. Revenge would be so sweet. She smiled to herself just thinking about it.

"This place sure has changed," Alex said, as he carried their drinks to a corner table. Several male couples were dancing together in front of the bandstand.

"I thought you might enjoy it."

He arched a brow as he turned back to her. "Even though you knew this place is now a gay bar?"

She shrugged, trying to act nonchalant. "It's obvious I don't know anything about you, Alex. Since you never tried to seduce me even once during our engagement, what else is a girl to think?"

His gaze narrowed on her. "I'll be more than

happy to show you just how much I want you, Paige."

The husky tenor of his voice told her he meant every word, sending a wave of heat through her body. But she wasn't about to back down. "I suppose an attempt to seduce me would be a way to evade the questions you still haven't answered."

"It would be more than an attempt," Alex promised her. "But I'll be happy to answer any questions before, during and after the seduction."

She reached for the vodka sour in front of her and took a deep swallow. Paige couldn't let him turn the tables on her, no matter how attractive she found him. He was a liar. A con artist. A jerk. She wanted to make him pay. But she also wanted information—and he'd just given her the perfect opening.

"Answering questions as foreplay," Paige mused, "that's innovative."

He leaned forward, his dark eyes hooded. "Ask away."

"Okay. You told me you started dating me a year ago to find out information about my stepfather," she began, "but you never told me why."

Alex reached for his glass of wine and took a long sip, long enough to formulate a vague answer to her question. "Stanley Weaver had done some work for my father's import company and we suspected him of stealing some sensitive information."

That hardly seemed plausible. Stanley Weaver had worked part-time as a delivery man for Bay

Bouquets, but as far as she knew, he hadn't moon-lighted for anyone else. "Exactly what kind of work did he do?"

"It's...complicated. I'd rather not go into it right now."

How convenient for him. It was becoming all too clear that breaking through Alex's defenses wouldn't be easy. She wanted him to open up to her. And to accomplish that, she needed him weak. She needed him vulnerable. There was only one way she knew of to get a man in that condition. Which meant she needed to plan a seduction of her own.

The idea appealed to her, even as she realized how easily it could backfire. Paige was all too aware that she wasn't immune to Alex's charms, despite the way he'd treated her. But why not satisfy her sexual curiosity and accomplish her goal at the same time?

The secret was to stay in control. To keep him off balance while she carefully plotted her course of action. If she played it just right, she could have him exactly where she wanted him—at her mercy.

"What do you want to talk about," she asked, tak-ing the straw out of her glass and running it slowly back and forth between her lips. She saw his gaze fall to her mouth and stay there, mesmerized by the movement.

He blinked, then met her gaze. "What?"

She leaned forward, dropping the straw back into

her glass. "Tell me something about the real Alex Mack."

"Okay," he agreed, setting back in his chair. "My full name is Alexander Stephen Mackopoulos."

She feigned surprise, not wanting to let on that she already knew that about him and more. "Then why did you tell me your name was Alex Mack?"

"To protect you." He hesitated. "And, I suppose, to protect myself as well. When I started dating you last year I was going to gather the information I needed about your stepfather, then get out of your life for good. Only it didn't work out that way."

"You succeeded in getting out of my life," she reminded him.

"But I'm back now," he countered. "Back to stay, if you'll let me."

He made it sound so easy. As if they could just pick up where they'd left off a year ago. Yet he hadn't mentioned anything about the time he'd spent in jail. Or the specific reason he'd been so desperate to find her stepfather that he'd feigned an engagement.

She wanted him desperate again. Desperate enough to do or say anything just to have her. "I don't want to rush into anything, Alex." She lowered her gaze. "I'm very...confused."

"Then let me make one thing very clear," he said softly. "Our past might have been a lie, Paige, but my feelings for you never were. I want us to have a new beginning. Starting right now."

Then Alex stood up and held out his hand. "Dance with me."

The band began to play a smoky blues song and she knew she couldn't have planned it better herself. Taking his hand, she rose to her feet and let him lead her to the dance floor.

The next moment she was in his arms, the familiar scent of his aftershave invading her senses. Her eyelids fluttered closed as she laid her head on his shoulder and they swayed together on the dance floor.

How many times had she dreamed of doing this after Alex had abandoned her? Only to wake up and have reality splash her in the face like a bucket of ice water.

"I've missed you," he murmured against her ear, his warm breath caressing her cheek.

How she wanted to believe him. How dangerous it would be to do so. Alex Mackopoulos wanted to draw her back under his spell and it wouldn't be too hard, judging by the way her body was reacting to his nearness. Paige needed to be very careful not to become entangled in the web she intended to weave for him.

"May I cut in?" asked a deep, male voice beside them.

They drew apart and Paige realized the band had already moved on to another song.

"It's up to the lady," Alex told the man.

Paige gave a shaky nod, needing some distance

from him to plan her next move. "Sure," she said, turning into the stranger's arms. But the man backed away from her in horror.

"I meant with him," the man said, jerking his thumb toward Alex.

"Sorry, I'm not available," Alex replied politely, unruffled by the invitation. Then he steered Paige off the dance floor and they wove through the crowd of patrons until they reached their table.

"Good thing I'm used to rejection," she quipped, reaching for her chair.

But Alex grasped her hand to keep her from sitting down. "Let's get out of here."

"And go where?"

"The parking lot. The beach. Hell, I don't care. I'll follow you anywhere, Paige."

"Anywhere?" she challenged, wondering if he'd overcome his fear of heights while he was in jail. That was one secret he hadn't been able to keep when they'd gone to the Space Needle together last year.

"Just lead the way."

"All right." Paige reached for her purse. "Let's go."

"DID I EVER MENTION that I'm not fond of heights?" Alex asked, feeling a little dizzy as he followed her up the ladder to the second-story roof of her house.

"Just don't look down," Paige said, reaching for the next rung.

Alex took her advice and looked up to see her firm, round bottom right in front of him. The snug fit of her slacks gave him a perfect view of the way it clenched and flexed with each step. So much temptation within easy reach of his hands made him feel even more dizzy.

At last they reached the top of the house and walked on to the flat portion of the roof that had been transformed into a garden. It was very private, very dark and very high off the ground.

"This garden is new," he said, warily peering over the edge. It was a long drop, with not so much as a tree or a shrub anywhere in sight to break a fall.

"I had some remodeling done a few months ago. Mom spends a lot of time up here looking at the sky—especially since Stanley pulled his disappearing act."

Alex turned around to face her. "So she still lives here with you?"

"Yes."

Margo Weaver had moved in with her daughter the day after her husband Stanley had disappeared. Her house, and especially the backyard, had given her bad vibes. Alex had been glad at the time, since he'd wanted access to both mother and daughter. But he'd come to genuinely like Margo, just as he'd found himself falling in love with her daughter.

"I live with my mother, too," he confided.

She looked up at him, surprised. "You do?"

He nodded. "Actually, she's my stepmother. But

she's my real mother in every sense of the word. I never knew my birth mother."

"She died?" Paige surmised, a flash of sympathy in her blue eyes.

"No, she got a better offer."

Her forehead crinkled. "I don't understand."

He took a deep breath, telling himself honesty was the only way to win her heart. No matter how painful he found the subject. "My father had an affair with his secretary twenty-nine years ago that resulted in a pregnancy. After I was born she showed up at his door and offered to sell me to him. He wanted to dicker on the price, but Thea put her foot down and demanded he pay the full amount in return for my birth mother giving up her parental rights."

"Thea?"

"His wife."

She took a moment to digest his story. "And she didn't divorce him or put rat poison in his coffee or anything?"

He shook his head, finding it hard to imagine a vengeful bone in his stepmother's body. "Thea is a very forgiving woman."

"More forgiving than I could ever be," Paige muttered to herself.

"Remind me never to drink your coffee," he said wryly.

A smile crossed her lips. "But that would defeat

the purpose, wouldn't it? I mean, if I really wanted revenge, I'd let you drink it without saying a word."

He took a step closer to her. "You don't want to poison me, do you, Paige? Or push me off the roof?"

She met his gaze. "I'd be lying if I said the thought hadn't crossed my mind."

He reached out to tuck a stray curl behind her ear, his fingers skimming the silky softness of her cheek. "I can think of a much better way to spend our time."

Desire clouded the blue depths of her eyes and her lips parted in an invitation he couldn't refuse. He leaned forward, but she pulled away from him at the last moment, deftly avoiding his kiss.

"Revenge is such a fascinating subject," she said, walking over to a telescope set up on the far end of the garden. "Let me show you."

Alex followed her there, the incline steeper on this section of the roof, so he had to concentrate to keep his balance.

Paige peered through the telescope lens, slowly adjusting the angle toward the canopy of stars in the night sky. "There it is. The belt of Orion."

"You know about the constellations?" he asked, finally reaching her side. His heart beat hard in his chest and he felt slightly off balance.

She turned to him. "When you are raised by a mother who is fascinated with UFOs, you learn all about the different lights in the sky. I even studied astronomy in college before I dropped out after my grandfather died."

"Why did you have to drop out?"

"Because running a business like Bay Bouquets is a full-time job," she replied. "My grandfather started with a tiny flower shop almost forty years ago and grew it into a thriving business. His dream was to keep it in the family and I'm the only Hanover he had left."

Alex stared at her. "I didn't know you went to college. Why haven't you mentioned this before?"

She shrugged, avoiding his gaze. "I guess the subject never came up during one of your interrogations."

He couldn't believe that was possible. Alex had dug into her past, into every detail of her life, during their time together. Or so he'd thought. Maybe he hadn't been the only one keeping secrets.

Watching Paige now as she peered once more through the telescope, he wondered if he'd ever really known her at all. "So, tell me about Orion."

"According to one version of Greek mythology," she said, turning to face him, "Orion was strong and handsome and spent a lot of time with Artemis, the virgin goddess of the hunt. When her twin brother Apollo noticed their relationship, he was jealous and decided to put an end to it."

"Brothers have a way of interfering," he muttered to himself.

"Apollo got his revenge by challenging Artemis

to prove her skill at archery," Paige continued. "He dared her to shoot at an object floating far out in sea. She hit the target with the first shot of her arrow, then discovered to her horror that she'd killed Orion. She went to Zeus and begged him to restore Orion's life, but he refused. So she put Orion's image in the heavens."

"That's it?" he said. "No happy ending?"

She looked up at him. "You believe in happy endings?"

"For some people." He took a step closer to her, knowing in his gut that she wanted him as much as he wanted her. Or maybe his mother was right and he had been in prison too long. "For us."

A hint of color washed up her cheeks, but she deftly changed the subject. "I'm surprised you've never heard that story before."

"Because I'm Greek?"

She tipped up her chin. "Because you're as handsome as Orion and as tempted as I am to shoot you with an arrow, I think I'd regret it as much as Artemis."

"So should I be afraid?"

"Yes," she said huskily, moving closer to him. "Be very afraid."

Then she kissed him.

It caught Alex completely off guard and he stumbled a little on the incline as she circled her arms around his neck and brought his mouth down to meet hers. But he quickly recovered his balance, if not his senses.

The hot, sweet taste of her mouth made him forget his fear of heights. Unlike their first courtship, Alex didn't have to hold anything back this time. He returned her kiss with the passion that had built up inside of him for one very long, very chaste year. A year he'd spent dreaming of a moment just like this.

It was over much too soon. Paige broke away from him with an enigmatic smile on her lips. "Good night, Alex."

Good night? She could kiss him like that and just walk away? Alex closed his eyes, waiting for the blood to return to his brain so he could think of something clever to say to make her stay.

But when he opened them again, she was already gone.

6

PAIGE RUSHED into the house and locked the door behind her. Not to keep Alex on the outside, but to keep herself inside. Her seduction trap had almost backfired on her.

Walking away from that kiss had been one of the hardest things she'd ever done. She sagged against the door, her muscles weak with passion.

He'd kissed her before but never quite like that—putting his whole heart and soul into it.

What if he really did want a fresh start? No ulterior motives? No games?

"No way," Paige muttered to herself, refusing to be duped again. Walking away from Alex tonight had been difficult, but definitely satisfying. And it was only the first step.

She was the one in control this time. Tomorrow she'd start researching Alex Mackopoulos and see if the things he'd told her about himself were true...and what other things he'd left out.

Margo walked into the living room, then faltered when she saw Paige standing there. "You startled me. I had no idea you'd be home so soon."

"Sorry," Paige replied, slipping her purse off her shoulder and setting it on the coffee table. "What did you do all evening?"

Margo smiled. "Well, I made a batch of popcorn and was all ready to watch the newest installment of *UFO Watch* when Ed Rooney showed up at the door."

Paige searched her memory, the name sounding vaguely familiar. "Ed who?"

"Ed Rooney," Margo reiterated. "The man I met at the flower shop today."

The invisible man. Now she remembered and it made her uncomfortable. "A customer just showed up at the door to our home uninvited? Where did he get the address? My house isn't listed in any telephone directory."

Margo gave a slight shrug. "I never thought to ask him. The show came on and I invited him in for a cup of coffee...."

"You invited him inside?" Paige echoed, not believing her ears. "A perfect stranger? Mom, what were you thinking?"

Margo bristled a little. "He wasn't a stranger. I met him in the store today and we were having a nice chat right before Alex walked in and I passed out."

"Alex didn't see anyone," Paige reminded her. "And neither did I."

"Well, Mr. Rooney was there," Margo insisted. "He told me tonight that an urgent appointment had prevented him from staying around until I regained consciousness. But he was very apologetic about it and we had a very nice visit."

Paige found herself desperately hoping it was true. Hoping that Ed Rooney really existed. She couldn't help but remember her mother's breakdown when Paige had been a teenager. How Margo had kept seeing her dead husband in crowds and hearing his voice.

"What did you talk to Mr. Rooney about?" Paige asked, hoping that her concern was unjustified.

"UFOs," Margo replied, picking up two empty cups off the coffee table. "Can you believe Ed knows more stories about aliens and cosmic abductions than I do? He's an expert on Roswell."

"Really?" She'd been giving her mother a lot of slack for her increasing UFO fascination ever since Stanley had disappeared. Even building her a garden on the roof. But what if something had finally pushed her over the edge? She hadn't started talking about this Mr. Rooney until Alex had shown up again. Was there a connection?

Paige sank down into a chair, too frazzled by her reaction to Alex's kiss to think clearly. She needed a good night's sleep. And a cold shower.

Margo headed toward the kitchen. "So how was your date?"

"Fine," Paige called after her.

A moment later, Margo was back in the living room. "Just fine? Is that all you have to say after re-

uniting with the man you love?" Then her brow
crinkled. "Or is Alex still suffering the aftereffects of
his amnesia? Does he even remember your relationship?"

"Better than I do," Paige muttered, referring to
the way he'd deceived her. "Look, Mom," she began, wanting to be truthful herself. "Alex never had
amnesia. That's not the reason he disappeared last
year."

Margo sat down on the sofa "I knew it. Alien abduction can cause memory blackouts. But that's
probably faded by now and it's all starting to come
back to him."

"No," Paige clarified. "His vanishing act had
nothing to do an alien abduction. He left of his own
free will."

"Then why is he back?"

Good question. He claimed he wanted another
chance with her and that kiss tonight had almost
proved it. "I'm not really sure. But I intend to find
out."

"You're making it all sound very mysterious."

"It's complicated," she said, repeating the excuse
Alex had given her tonight.

"Love always is," Margo said with a wistful sigh.
"I told myself I'd never give up waiting for Stanley
to come back to me. But now…"

Paige saw a glimmer of hope for her mother's future. If this Rooney character was real. "Now Ed
Rooney is making you have second thoughts?"

"Exactly," Margo replied. "Is that disloyal of me?"

"I'd say it's smart. You've put your life on hold long enough."

"Not that Ed has made any romantic overtures," Margo said hastily. "But he does seem interested in me."

Paige smiled at the pink blush on her mother's cheeks. "That's a good sign."

"What about Alex?" Margo asked her.

"What about him?"

Margo frowned. "Why do you keep repeating my questions? You're being awfully evasive tonight, Paige. I get the feeling that something is bothering you."

She'd learned evasiveness from a pro. But her mother was right, something was bothering her. That kiss. Or more specifically, her reaction to it. Maybe she'd better rethink her strategy.

"I'm sorry," Paige said at last. "I'm just confused because I'm not sure what's going to happen between me and Alex."

"Maybe you should ask yourself what you *want* to happen."

That was easy. Paige wanted to believe in Alex again. To trust him. But that was impossible now. "I think I need to sleep on it."

"Good idea. Just don't wait too long to make up your mind or he might disappear again."

"I won't let that happen," she vowed. And she

knew the best way to prevent it was to find out everything she could about Alex Mackopoulos. His home. His business. His personal life. All the things he'd kept from her the first time around.

She'd strip him naked. Figuratively speaking.

THREE DAYS LATER, Paige arrived at the Mackopoulos house. It was located in an exclusive suburb just outside of San Francisco. A Tudor-style home, she'd found the address while conducting an extensive search about the Mackopoulos family at the local library and the county courthouse.

What she had discovered fascinated her. Alex's father and stepmother had both immigrated from Greece when they were very young, their families settling near each other in Southern California. Lucian Mackopoulos had been an entrepreneur, specializing in Greek imports. Thea Mackopoulos was a devoted housewife and mother, dedicating more time to volunteer organizations than most people spend at a full-time job.

Paige had read archived newspaper articles about Alex's scholarship to Cal Tech and his brother Nico's accomplishments on the high school football field. She'd come across their father Lucian's obituary, noting his death had taken place only a few months ago.

She'd found herself wondering if Alex had been released from jail for the funeral, then realized there was still too much she didn't know. So now she was ready to gather some firsthand information.

Starting by calling the house this morning to see if Alex was there. When the maid told her he'd be out all day, she knew this was the perfect opportunity to meet his mother. She'd even come up with a way to do it.

Paige was intrigued by a woman who would take her husband's illegitimate child into her home. Did Thea Mackopoulos know about Alex's broken engagement or had he been keeping secrets from her, too?

The maid met her at the front door, then showed her into the large living room. But instead of finding Thea waiting for her, there was a man standing by the window who bore a striking resemblance to Alex.

"Hello," he said, turning toward her as she walked into the room. "I'm Nico Mackopoulos."

She hadn't expected Alex's half brother to look so much like him. He shared the same square jaw and bold nose. The same hooded eyes, though Nico's were gray instead of brown. His hair was a shade lighter, too.

"I'm from Bay Bouquets," she said, purposely avoiding using her name. She reached out to shake his hand. It was big and warm, just like the man himself.

Recognition dawned in his eyes. "Bay Bouquets. I

think I've driven by your shop before. Are you the owner?"

"Yes, I am," she replied, finding herself answering questions instead of asking them. "I was hoping to see Mrs. Mackopoulos today."

"She's out at the moment," Nico said. "But maybe I can help you."

Paige didn't have any choice now but to go through with the charade. She couldn't think of any other credible explanation for being here. "Actually, I just wanted to tell her that she's the lucky winner of one month's supply of fresh flowers, delivered to her door every week."

He arched a brow. "Really? I don't recall her entering a drawing."

"The pool is made up of my former customers," Paige explained. "It's a promotional tool. We did some business a couple of years ago with Mackopoulos Imports."

Paige had discovered that fact late last night when she'd been unable to sleep. The Mackopoulos name had nagged at her, seeming oddly familiar. It had finally driven her out of bed to scour all her old business records until she'd finally found it.

Lucian Mackopoulos had contracted Bay Bouquets for the sale and maintenance of several indoor plants in the executive offices and lobby of his company. The service contracts usually ran six months, but according to her records, Lucian had never renewed.

The business connection made her even more curious about Alex's involvement with her stepfather. Stanley Weaver had delivered plants and flowers for Bay Bouquets, as well as provided maintenance services, such as watering and trimming dead leaves in several office buildings. Had Alex met him that way?

"I'm sure my mother will be thrilled with her prize," Nico said. "She loves flowers."

Paige hesitated, not quite knowing what else to say and disappointed that she would not be meeting Alex's mother today. Fortunately, her backup plan gave her an excuse to be here next week. And the week after that. "Do you mind if I bring the flowers in now?"

He looked surprised. "You have them with you?"

"They're in the delivery van."

"Sure. Let me help you," Nico offered, following her out of the room.

"Thanks," she replied. "I'd appreciate that."

Nico Mackopoulos was as handsome as Alex, but in a different, more polished way. He was more sturdily built, looking more like a man of leisure than his leaner brother.

"You have a beautiful home, Mr. Mackopoulos," she said when he caught her staring at him.

He smiled. "I insist that you call me Nico."

"Only if you call me Paige."

He nodded, taking no special notice of her name. "It would be my pleasure."

Alex must have kept his family in the dark about her. Hardly surprising given his methods.

"Have you lived here long?" she asked Nico, striving to keep the conversation going between them.

"All of my life," he replied. "My mother talked about selling the house after my father died, but Alex and I finally talked her out of the idea."

She opened the back of the van, careful to keep her voice neutral. "Alex?"

"My brother," he informed her. "The black sheep of the family."

"Why do you say that?" she asked, pulling out a large floral arrangement and handing it to him.

"There are so many reasons," he said with a sigh. "I really don't know where to begin."

They walked toward the house together, each carrying a vase full of flowers.

"I suppose every family has a black sheep or two," Paige said, hoping to steer Nico back to the subject of his brother.

"But few of them have been in jail."

She stumbled going up the step and he grasped her arm to steady her.

"Are you all right?" he asked, his gray eyes sweeping down her body for a moment before meeting her gaze once again.

"I'm fine, thank you." Paige couldn't believe he'd come right out and told her about Alex's jail time. This was the kind of information she wanted. And judging by Nico's affability, this was the place to get it.

They set the vases down on a table in the foyer, then made another trip to the van.

"I imagine your brother's incarceration must have been difficult on your entire family," Paige ventured.

Nico nodded. "Especially my mother. She's always seen the good in Alex. I, on the other hand, have seen his...darker side."

"That sounds ominous," she replied, more curious than ever as she unloaded the third and fourth vases of fresh flowers from the van.

He chuckled. "I suppose it does. Don't get me wrong, Alex isn't evil. He just knows how to manipulate people to his own advantage."

Paige couldn't believe Nico was talking this way about his own brother. She opened her mouth to defend her former fiancé, then closed it again, realizing what Nico had said was true. Alex had certainly manipulated her for his own advantage.

"Is that why he went to jail," she asked, wanting more details, "for manipulating the wrong person?"

He pushed open the front door for her, then followed Paige inside the house. "I really shouldn't be airing the family's dirty laundry in front of a stranger."

Nico set down his vase, then took the one she was holding out of her hands. "But for some reason, you don't seem like a stranger."

Her breath caught in her throat as he took a step closer to her. Was Alex's brother actually flirting with her?

"It's not often I meet a woman who is so easy to talk to," he continued, "and so easy to look at."

A guilty blush crept unbidden up her cheeks. But why should she feel guilty? She didn't owe Alex anything. Nico seemed like an honest, kind gentleman. A real rarity these days and a man any woman would find attractive. Paige was certain she would too, once she stopped comparing him to Alex.

"Forgive me if I've made you uncomfortable," Nico said, backing away from her a step. "Sometimes I get carried away in the presence of a beautiful woman."

"No," she said, breaking her stunned silence. "I'm flattered. Really."

A smile tipped up the corners of his mouth. "Then perhaps you'll consider having dinner with me sometime."

"I'd love to," she replied, before she had time for any second thoughts.

His smile widened. "Are you free Friday evening?"

"I think so," she replied, a nervous flutter in her stomach. Paige hadn't gone out on a real date since...before Alex.

"Wonderful." He reached into the drawer of the desk behind him and drew out a pencil and paper.

"Write down your address for me. I'll pick you up at eight o'clock."

She hesitated a moment, then scribbled down the address of the time-share apartment she was leasing from Franco during the weekends. That way she wouldn't have to explain to her mother why she was dating Alex's brother. Especially since she wasn't quite sure herself.

Paige headed toward the door, still facing Nico. "Well, I hope your mother enjoys the flowers."

"I'm sure she will." He folded up the square of paper she'd handed him and slipped it into his shirt pocket. "I'm looking forward to Friday, Paige."

"Me, too."

But by the time she was in the van, Paige had a feeling she'd made a terrible mistake. Wanting revenge on Alex was one thing. Getting it by dating his brother was quite another. It wouldn't be fair to Nico or to herself. She'd have to tell him the truth when he came to pick her up Friday night.

But what if it didn't matter to him? What if he still wanted to date her?

Then...she'd have a big decision to make. On the positive side, dating the Mackopoulos brothers might be good for her battered ego.

Even if it wasn't good for her heart.

7

PAIGE RETURNED to Bay Bouquets to find Alex standing alone in the front of the store. She looked toward the back, but could see no sign of her mother.

"What are you doing here?" she asked, flustered by the fact that she'd just accepted a date with his brother.

"Waiting for you." Alex rounded the counter. "I'd like to take you out to lunch today if you're free."

She hadn't seen him since the night she'd kissed him on the roof, avoiding his phone calls while she collected background information on him.

Knowledge was power and Paige was finding out more about Alex every day. She had told herself that her irrational attraction to him would diminish the more she got to know him.

But the opposite seemed to be true.

Which just proved that she couldn't carry this charade on too long. She'd gotten off to a good start the other night on the roof. Now it was time to kick her plan into high gear. To make him want her enough to tell her anything.

Then she could leave him.

"Your place or mine?" she asked, stepping closer to him.

Heat flared in his dark brown eyes. "Actually, I want to take you someplace special. It's a surprise, but I think you'll like it."

Desire for him curled through her, unbidden and unwanted. Paige steeled herself against it even as her gaze drank in his powerful body. She'd dreamed about him again last night, her subconscious giving free rein to her fantasies. His hands had been all over her, touching and enticing. Relentless in their sensual exploration until at last she'd awoken trembling with need for him.

Not a good sign. Seducing Alex would only be a success if she remained detached. A difficult prospect, judging by the way her body hummed even now at his nearness. But not impossible. She just had to remember how he'd hurt her. And why she could never give him the opportunity to do it again.

"I'll just let Mom know we're leaving," she said, heading toward the back.

"She's not here."

Paige turned to face him. "Where is she?"

He grinned. "Out on a date. She was very excited about meeting some guy named Ed for coffee. So I offered to watch the front counter for her until you got back."

Paige's heart sank. "Ed Rooney?"

Alex cocked a brow. "You don't like him?"

"I don't even know him." *Or know if he exists.* Maybe now was the time to find out. "Did she happen to mention where she was meeting him?"

"The Drip on Burlington. She said she'd be back here in an hour." He glanced at his watch. "I'd guess she left about thirty minutes ago."

Paige whirled around and headed for the back storeroom. "Then I might still have time to catch him."

"Catch who?" Alex asked.

But Paige didn't stop to answer his question. She found Lena, her part-time clerk, in the back unloading a delivery of fresh carnations and asked her to watch the store. Then she hurried out the side door and headed east on the sidewalk. With the midday traffic, she knew it would be faster to walk the six blocks to The Drip rather than drive and try to find a parking spot.

A moment later, Paige noticed Alex walking up beside her. "What are you doing here?"

"Trying to figure out what's going on," he said, matching her stride. "I don't think I've ever seen you this upset before."

"You should have seen me the day you left me at the altar," she said wryly.

Paige didn't want to share her fears about her mother with him, so she'd given him a flip answer instead. Now she regretted it. Why did she have to keep reminding him how much he'd hurt her? It just made her look weak.

Alex didn't say anything for half a block. But when he did finally speak, the sincerity in his tone broke through her defenses. "I'm sorry for everything I did to you, Paige. For hurting you. I can't go back and fix the past. Believe me, there are a lot of things I would change in my life if I could."

"Like what?" she asked, wondering if he meant his stint in jail.

"Leaving you last year tops the list. Then there's my career. I'm a financial manager and I love my work, but instead of taking a job with the family business, I should have gone out on my own."

"What stopped you?"

A muscle flexed in his jaw. "When you're the bastard of the family, you always feel like you have to prove your loyalty."

Prove his loyalty to whom, she wondered. His parents? His brother? Nico had referred to him as a black sheep. Maybe Alex had been fighting for acceptance all his life.

"I think that's normal in any family," she mused. "I quit college to fulfill my grandfather's dream of taking over his business. Don't get me wrong," she added hastily. "I like it well enough. But running a flower shop wouldn't have been my first career choice."

"You wanted to be an astronomer," he surmised as they stopped at a street corner and waited for the light to change. "To study the stars."

"I still do," Paige said, surprised to find herself

confiding in him. "I've started going to night school to earn my bachelor's degree."

"Good for you." The admiration in his eyes gave her a warm thrill of pleasure.

"It probably won't come to anything. I'll still have the flower shop to run. But maybe someday..." Her voice trailed off and she looked up to find herself staring at his mouth.

She remembered all too well the feel of that mouth on her own. The hard length of his body against hers as they'd clung to each other on the rooftop. She should have ripped his clothes off and made love to Alex right there. Gotten him completely out of her system.

"Paige?"

She blinked. "Yes?"

"If you keep looking at me like that, we're not going to make it to the coffee shop."

She stepped away from him, horrified that she'd been that obvious. Then again, she *wanted* him to think she was attracted to him.

But Paige couldn't fool herself, even as she planned to fool Alex. She *was* attracted to him. There was no use denying the obvious. But now wasn't the time or the place to act on it. Not when she had to deal with the very real possibility that her mother might be headed for another breakdown.

The aroma of freshly ground coffee filled the air when they arrived at The Drip. The coffeehouse served most of its patrons in an outdoor courtyard filled with small, round tables. Most of them were already occupied.

"I don't see her," Alex said as they made a slow circle around the perimeter of the courtyard.

"There she is!" Paige exclaimed, hiding behind a wide post and pulling Alex with her. "Do you see her? She's right next to the giant coffee cup."

"Is there a reason we're hiding?" Alex whispered against her ear, his body pressed against her in a most distracting way.

"I don't want her to see us."

"I already figured that out. Now do you mind telling me why?"

Paige did mind, but she desperately wanted another opinion before she made a complete fool of herself. Judging from the expressions of some of the customers staring at them, it was already too late.

She looked up at him. "Do you remember that day in the flower shop when my mother fainted?"

He nodded. "Margo took one look at me and thought I'd fallen out of the sky."

"You were real," Paige affirmed, "but I'm not so sure about the other man my mother claimed she saw in Bay Bouquets that day."

"She did mention someone," he murmured, his brow furrowed in thought. "What was his name again?"

"Mr. Rooney. Ed Rooney."

He nodded, comprehension dawning in his eyes. "The same Ed she's meeting today?"

"If there is an Ed." Paige craned her neck around the post to look at her mother. Margo sat alone at her table, a cup of coffee in front of her. Another cup of steaming coffee sat in front of the empty chair beside her.

"You think she's created a make-believe boyfriend for herself?" Alex asked, sounding skeptical.

"I don't know anything for sure," Paige replied honestly. "And I hope more than anything that it's not true. But she does have a history of...problems. And I've seen enough signs to wonder if Ed Rooney is simply a figment of my mother's imagination."

"Margo is not crazy," he said firmly.

Paige wanted desperately to believe him, but the facts kept getting in the way. "I hope you're right. When Stanley first disappeared, I thought she latched on to that alien abduction theory as a way to cope with his abandonment. But she just won't let it go. My mother really believes that stuff, Alex. She even went on some ridiculous cable television show called *UFO Watch* to tell her story. Worse, she dragged our relationship into it, convinced you would only leave me against your will."

"She was right," he said softly.

His words caught her off guard, but Paige let his comment pass. If she tried to delve into its meaning she might risk going crazy, too.

"My mother keeps talking about this Ed Rooney," she continued, "but I've never, ever seen the man. He never shows up when I'm around. Never calls when I'm home to hear the telephone ring. It just doesn't add up."

"Those could all be coincidences," Alex countered. "Margo might be a little...eccentric, but I'm sure she's perfectly sane."

"Then who is she talking to right now?" Paige asked, pointing toward her mother's table.

He turned to see her chatting animatedly to the empty chair. "No one."

Paige closed her eyes as dread circled her heart. "This can't be happening."

Alex pulled her into his arms, the warmth of his big, strong body more comforting than she wanted to admit.

"Maybe there's a reasonable explanation," he said, his lips moving against her hair.

"What should I do?" Paige asked, feeling more helpless than she ever had in her life. "I mean, is it safe for her to even be out on the street? Could she get hurt?"

"Let's go talk to her," Alex said, leading her out from behind the post, "and find out."

Margo's green eyes widened with surprise when she saw them approach. "I didn't expect to see you two here."

"Mom, what are *you* doing here?" Paige asked, her throat tight.

"Waiting for Ed to come back. He had to go make a private call in his car."

Paige took a deep breath, deciding to face this

problem head-on. "We saw you talking to the chair."

A flush mottled Margo's cheeks. "Well, this is embarrassing." She leaned forward and lowered her voice. "If you must know, it's been awhile since I've been out on a date. I was rehearsing some fun and fascinating things to talk to Ed about. But certainly not loud enough for anyone to hear me."

Alex gave Paige a look, as if to say there'd been a reasonable explanation after all. But she wasn't completely convinced.

"You've never told me what Ed looks like," Paige persisted, wanting to get to the truth.

"You've never asked," Margo countered. "In fact, I noticed that it seems to bother you when I talk about him, so lately I've tried to avoid the subject."

"I don't want you to do that," she said, feeling guilty now. "I really am interested."

"I think you'd like him, Paige," Margo confided. "He's in his mid-fifties and quite distinguished. Dark hair with just a touch of silver at the temples." A smile curved her lips. "And he has the most amazing blue eyes."

"I'd like to meet him," Paige said, her belief that Rooney didn't exist wavering a bit. Alex was right, her mother seemed perfectly sane. Maybe Paige was the one imagining things.

Hardly surprising, given the stress she'd been under lately. Trying to tempt Alex while fighting off her own feelings for him. She could feel the emotional barriers she'd built up against him slowly eroding with each passing day. Her common sense under constant assault by her hormones.

"I think it's a little premature to introduce him to my daughter," Margo said. "After all, this is only our first official date. I don't want to scare him away."

"Maybe we could all go out to dinner together," Alex suggested. "A double date."

Paige wasn't sure she liked the way he spoke for both of them. Or the way his hand hovered at her waist, the tips of his broad fingers pressed lightly against her back. It brought to mind her erotic dreams again and her skin began to tingle with anticipation, aching for more of his touch.

Margo nodded. "I like that idea."

"How about Friday night?" Alex asked, turning to Paige.

She moved out of his reach so she could think, then remembered the date she'd just made with his brother. How could she have let everything become so complicated? "I'm afraid I've already got plans."

"What kind of plans?" Margo asked.

"At my apartment," she improvised. "I need to work on a big project that's due in one of my classes next week."

"Then how about Saturday?" Margo said. "I could ask Ed and we could all go out to dinner." She looked up at Alex. "Unless you think it's too pushy for a woman to ask a man out so early in the relationship."

"Not at all," he replied, his gaze on Paige now. "Most men like it when a woman takes charge."

That was good to know, since Paige intended to go on the offensive as soon as possible. She needed to feel in control again. To remember why she'd started playing this dangerous game with Alex in the first place. Though it wasn't so much about revenge anymore, but understanding.

Alex had lied to her for a reason that had something to do with her stepfather. Stanley Weaver's disappearance had driven her mother to search the sky for UFOs and to talk to empty chairs. If Alex had some clue that could possibly lead to Stanley, then Paige needed to know it. No matter how she had to obtain the information.

"All right, I'll ask him out Saturday night," Margo announced. Then she waved them away from her table. "Now shoo before Ed comes back. I don't want him to know we've been talking about him behind his back."

Paige hesitated, reluctant to leave before seeing for herself that Ed Rooney really existed. But Saturday was only a few days away. She could at least give her mother that much benefit of the doubt.

"I'll see you back at the shop," Paige said.

"I'll be there soon," Margo promised.

Alex waited until they were out of her mother's

earshot, then said, "Do you want me to stick around and see if anyone shows up?"

She shook her head. "I don't want to start spying on her, especially since I'm probably the one imagining things. It's been a stressful week."

"Thanks to me."

She looked up at him, not able to deny it. "Yes."

"Then let me make it up to you with that special lunch that I promised." Alex turned toward the street and hailed them a taxi.

"I really should get back to the shop," she said, not sure what to expect. "I need to check the inventory and study for a physics quiz and..."

"You're coming with me," Alex interjected, opening the cab door, "and I won't take no for an answer."

She hesitated. "Where exactly are we going?"

"Get in and you'll see."

Her curiosity overcame her hesitation. She climbed into the cab, Alex following behind her.

"Destination?" the driver asked.

"La Belle on Market Street," Alex directed him.

Paige knew she had to be hearing things. That was one of the most exclusive spas on the West Coast. "You're taking me to La Belle for lunch? They don't even have food there."

He smiled as the cab pulled away from the curb. "Don't worry, Paige. I guarantee that when we leave La Belle you'll be completely satisfied."

8

ALEX MIGHT NOT BE ABLE to change the mistakes he'd
made in the past, but he could show Paige how well
he planned to treat her in the future. He sat in the
well-appointed cocktail lounge of La Belle Spa, sipping an iced tea while the woman he loved received
a hot-stone massage.

Tony Wang, the owner of the spa and a good
friend, walked into the lounge. "Nice to see you
again, Mack. And hey, my condolences about your
father."

"Thank you," Alex stood up to shake his hand.
He and Tony had roomed in the same dorm together at Cal Tech. Now Alex worked part-time as
his financial manager. A job which had several
perks, including a standing appointment at La Belle
available to him any day of the week.

He rarely took advantage of it, but today was an
exception. Ever since he'd kissed Paige on the rooftop, he hadn't been able to get her out of his mind.
Hell, he was going out of his mind with wanting
her. And every time he looked into her eyes, he saw
his own feelings reflected there. The desire as well

as the apprehension. But most of all, the overwhelming need.

So Alex had finally decided to do something about it. His countless apologies for the past seemed to have no effect on her. She didn't believe him anyway. Paige might not trust him yet, but he knew she wasn't immune to him, either. Now he planned to show her just how much he cared with actions rather than words.

"How are things going?" Tony asked. His friend had kept in regular contact during Alex's confinement in jail, adamantly refusing to hire another financial manager for La Belle. Tony had only wanted the best for his business and had insisted Alex was it. So Alex had worked from his jail cell, keeping track of the books and making investment suggestions for the spa, grateful for something to keep him busy.

"Better all the time," Alex replied, wondering how much longer he had to wait until Paige was ready for him to join her. "How's Jolene?"

Tony grinned. "Pregnant."

"Hey, congratulations," Alex said, slapping him on the back. "You two will make great parents."

Tony laughed. "I wasn't even sure I'd make a decent husband, but marriage has been even better than I expected. Forget the horror stories you hear, Alex. I think you should give it a shot."

"I need to find a willing woman first."

Tony held up a key. "May I suggest the woman in

suite twelve? I believe she's waiting to dine with you."

"I owe you," Alex replied, taking the key out of his hands. "Thanks for making an exception and letting me bring a catered lunch into your spa."

"My pleasure," Tony said. "I might even co-opt the idea and offer my patrons a Lovers' Luncheon Special—massage included."

Alex definitely liked that idea, though he and Paige weren't lovers—yet.

"Hey, before you go," Tony called after him. "Keep a day open next week for a long meeting. The entire day, if you have the time."

Alex forced himself to stop and turn around. "Is there a problem?"

Tony grinned. "Just the opposite. I hope to make you an offer no sane man would refuse."

Curiosity battled with his desire to see Paige. "What kind of offer?"

"I'm expanding the business," Tony replied. "Right now I plan to build more La Belle Spas along the California coast, but who knows? I might go nationwide before I'm through. And I'd really like you to sign on for a permanent, full-time position."

The idea appealed to Alex. Working for his father had been one thing, but Alex knew he and Nico would never make good business partners. Nico could have Mackopoulos Imports and Alex could pursue a career and a life all his own. *A life with Paige.*

"I'll definitely give it some thought," Alex said. "Go ahead and set up a meeting. I'll be there."

"Good. And bring your lady over to my place sometime. I know Jolene would love to meet her."

"I'll see what I can do." He knew Paige would like Tony's pretty, petite wife, but first Alex had to make her like *him*. That wouldn't be easy, given their history. But a Mackopoulos never surrendered—or backed away from a challenge.

Tony stepped closer, lowering his voice. "And may I suggest purchasing a bottle of Strawberry Magic, one of our custom massage oils. It's quite popular with our female clientele."

If only it were that simple. Alex knew it would take more than magic oil to win Paige's heart. He'd have to work for it.

THE HOT-STONE MASSAGE had cleared Paige's head as much as it had soothed her body. Easing the tension that had filled her since Alex had reappeared in her life and her mother had become obsessed with Mr. Rooney.

The masseuse had just left, but she couldn't seem to summon the energy to get up and get dressed. Paige lay on her stomach on a narrow padded table, her eyes closed and her entire body still boneless from the massage. Soft jazz played over the suite's speakers and she drifted on a wave of pure relaxation.

She floated into her familiar dream about Alex.

His hands were stroking her body once again, strong and skillful. She breathed a soft sigh of satisfaction as they moved up her back and over her bare shoulders.

His fingers gently kneaded the muscles above her shoulder blades, then eased over the curve of her spine, taking their sweet time as a fire began to burn deep inside of her.

"Feel good?" he asked.

"Mmmmm," she murmured, barely registering the fact that her dream lover had spoken to her. He'd never done it before. Only touched her. Inflamed her.

Just like he was doing now.

Paige slowly opened her eyes and found that she wasn't dreaming at all. Alex stood beside the massage table as his incredible hands glided over her smooth back.

"I couldn't resist," he said huskily, his hands still moving on her. "Tell me to stop and I will."

But she couldn't say a word, her eyes fluttering closed again as she got caught up in a sensual haze that made it impossible to think at all. She could only feel as he drew his broad hands slowly down the length of her back. Then he slid them over her spine, lingering at the narrow slope of her waist.

Heat pooled low in her body as his hands slipped around her rib cage, his fingertips just brushing the sides of her breasts. They tingled beneath her and a low moan escaped her throat, making it impossible to pretend she was still asleep.

"So beautiful," he breathed, leaning down to skim his lips over the back of her neck.

Paige turned around to stop him and found herself kissing him instead, clutching the back of his head to her with one hand and the towel to her chest with the other. All her revenge plans melted in the heat of his mouth. She didn't know who was seducing who and found she didn't care.

As long as he didn't stop touching her.

He granted her silent wish, one hand slipping beneath the towel and finding her breast. His fingers, slick with the massage oil, slid over and around her taut nipples.

"Please," she gasped against his mouth as his fingers continued to stroke her. Driving her beyond herself, beyond anything she'd ever experienced before.

"Please what?" he whispered, his mouth hovering over her lips.

"Please...don't stop."

He kissed her again, loving the way she tasted of strawberries and tequila from the margarita the spa had served her when they'd first arrived.

Alex had skipped the drink, but now found himself almost drunk with desire for her. Deepening the kiss, he savored the dance of her tongue in his mouth as his hands explored her body.

Then he moved his mouth lower.

She leaned back on the padded table, letting his lips burn a trail down her throat. All the while, his fingers strummed her breasts, now as slick with oil as his hands.

Then he replaced his fingers with his mouth, tasted the strawberry-flavored massage oil and the unparalleled sweetness of Paige. He swirled his tongue around one nipple, then gently closed his lips over the peak, applying just enough pressure to make her moan for more.

Alex lingered there for a while, until her hands tangled in his hair and moved his head to her other breast. He lavished it with his tongue while his hand slid slowly down the length of her flat belly and slipped underneath the towel at her waist.

The scent of strawberries mingled with the scent of her desire, a heady combination that made his own flesh strain against his slacks.

His fingertips brushed the silk of her panties, then burrowed underneath to touch the soft curls at the apex of her thighs. When she arched into his hand, he moved it even lower.

"Alex," she cried, her breath catching in her throat.

He raised his head from her breast, stilling his fingers inside of her. He wouldn't take her where she didn't want to go. "Do you want me to stop, Paige?"

"Don't stop," she gasped, flexing her hips against his hand. *"Please, don't stop."*

He loved watching her face as his fingers moved

once more, parting the silken flesh to find the bud of her desire. He leaned down to kiss her lips, capturing her soft cries in his mouth. Her hands grasped his shoulders as she thrashed beneath his touch.

"That's right," he whispered, his fingers moving deeper. "Hold on to me."

The sight of her passion inflamed him more than he ever thought possible. Then she came undone in his arms.

Alex burned to bury himself inside of her and share those sensual vibrations. The bulge in his slacks brushed against her bare thigh and the inadvertent contact wrenched a tortured groan from low in his chest.

"Do you want me to stop?" he asked huskily, repeating the refrain as his lust-clouded brain debated whether to make love to her on the massage table or the floor.

"Yes."

It took a moment for the word to register in his mind. When it did, he swallowed another groan, this one of frustration. Alex took three deep breaths, his body taking even longer to comprehend her meaning.

At last he moved away from her, clumsily covering her back up with the thick towel. "I'll wait for you outside."

Then he turned and walked out the door.

WHAT HAD SHE DONE?

Her plan to seduce him had completely backfired. She'd been the one who had lost control, actually begging him not to stop touching her. The one desperate for the sweet release his fingers had promised her.

Paige climbed off the massage table, her body still tingling and her mind spinning. So much for her detachment. Her strategy to act like she wanted him until she got her answers. Only she hadn't been acting just now. Her reaction was all too real and it shook her to her very core.

But it wasn't just his hands that had moved her. It was the love she'd seen shining in his dark eyes. Something she assumed Alex couldn't fake. *Or could he?* Paige simply wasn't sure anymore.

She took a deep breath, then another. This was not a catastrophe. Alex was the one who had surprised her with a massage, catching her off guard when she was half-asleep. Not that protesting had even crossed her mind once he'd started touching her. He had great hands. *Incredible hands.*

Hands that could almost make her forget Alex still hadn't revealed his past to her or made any plans for the future. At least she hadn't let him go any further, though she'd seen the evidence of his impressive arousal with her own eyes.

After combing shaky fingers through her tousled hair, she placed her palms on her warm cheeks. Everything smelled like strawberries. Paige took a moment to hastily straighten her clothes, then walked out of suite twelve. Alex wasn't in the hallway, but a receptionist saw her and waved her down.

"Mr. Mackopoulos is waiting to dine with you in a private suite," the tiny Asian woman informed her. "Just follow this hallway and take your first right."

"Thank you," Paige said, dreading the thought of facing him again so soon. *So why do it?*

"Miss," she called after the woman.

The receptionist turned. "Yes?"

"How much do I owe you for today?"

"No charge," she said with a smile. "Mr. Mackopoulos has promised to take care of everything."

He already had. But Paige didn't want to be beholden to him for anything. Not now. Not ever.

Digging into her purse, she retrieved her checkbook. "I'd rather pay for it myself."

"Very well." The receptionist led her to a desk and sifted through a wicker basket before handing her a copy of the invoice.

Paige almost dropped her checkbook when she saw the total amount. But she wrote out the check anyway, telling herself to transfer some funds from savings so she didn't overdraw her checking account.

She tore off the check, then handed it to the receptionist. "Please tell Mr. Mackopoulos I've decided to find my own way home."

"Yes, ma'am."

Paige exited La Belle through a side door, then

walked out into the street to grab a taxi. She'd need some time alone to think before she saw Alex again.

Time to figure out what she really wanted.

A COLD SHOWER didn't help. Neither did burying himself in work. Alex sat in his office at Mackopoulos Imports, his desk full of financial summaries, but his mind and body consumed with Paige. Six hours ago he'd held her in his arms at La Belle Spa, believing he'd finally reached past her defenses.

Until she'd told him to stop.

Walking out of that suite had been one of the hardest things he'd ever done. Because he knew, down into his soul, that she'd wanted him. Her body couldn't lie, even if Paige was trying to fool herself into believing that he was all wrong for her.

That's why she'd left La Belle Spa without him, leaving Alex alone, aroused and frustrated as hell. Six hours later, he was still frustrated. Still aroused, too, every time he thought of the way her luscious body had responded to him.

He knew making love to her would be even better. Paige knew it, too. That's why she'd panicked. Letting all her doubts and fears cloud what seemed so perfectly clear to him.

They belonged together.

Alex didn't even question it anymore. Not after what happened today. But they couldn't move forward until she forgave him for the past. And he didn't know how to make that happen.

A knock sounded on the door, tearing his thoughts away from Paige. "Come in."

Thea walked inside, carrying a wicker basket on her arm. "I brought you some dinner."

He tossed down his pen, giving up the charade of working. "You didn't have to do that, Mom."

"I wanted to do it." She set the basket down on his desk and began unloading it. "I used to bring meals here for your father sometimes. I miss that. I miss him."

"So do I," Alex admitted, clearing a space in front of him as she unwrapped roast lamb sandwiches. He suddenly realized Thea Mackopoulos knew all about forgiveness. She'd taken her husband back after he'd cheated on her. Even accepted his bastard son into her home and family.

"Now tell me what's bothering you," she said, pulling another chair up to the desk.

He looked up from his sandwich. "Nothing."

"Please. I know my sons. Is this about business?"

"No, it's...personal."

She handed him a paper napkin. "Then it's about Paige Hanover."

Alex had forgotten he'd told his mother her name. He'd left out all the other details, certain she wouldn't approve of the way he'd treated Paige last year. He didn't like it himself. "I screwed up. And I'm not sure how to fix it."

Thea didn't ask him for details. She'd always respected the private lives of her sons, reserving her opinion unless they asked for it. "Is she worth the trouble to fix it?"

He didn't even hesitate. "Yes."

"Then you do what your father did twenty-nine years ago," she said, her voice wistful. "Admit you made a horrible mistake and vow never to do it again. Then you live that vow every day, showing her why she's worth it. Before long, she'll start to believe it."

Alex couldn't meet her gaze, knowing his father hadn't lived up to his vow. That blackmail tape proved it. A tape he hoped like hell never fell into his mother's hands.

"Or you could bring her by the house and I could tell Paige how wonderful you are and that you deserve a second chance." Thea smiled at him. "Would that work?"

He laughed. "I don't think so."

"Well, the offer's open if you ever need it."

"Thanks, Mom." He leaned over and kissed her cheek. "And thanks for the sandwiches."

He didn't know whether it was the food or the advice that made him feel better, but after she left, Alex started thinking about what his mother had said. Winning Paige back couldn't be accomplished in a single day. There was no quick fix that could make her trust him again. He'd have to put in the time and the commitment to prove his love.

Today had just been a start. A very good start. It had proved Paige wasn't immune to him. Now he needed to press that advantage every chance he got.

9

Franco's Notes:

I FINALLY CONVINCED Paige to wear the skirt for her
big date tonight. When will people realize that gay
men have the best taste in clothes? My work is never
done. At least I'll have another opportunity to see
the skirt in action.

Things got pretty wild around here the last time
she wore it, with Paige calling the police on that big
Greek who kept banging on her door. Apparently,
tonight's date isn't the same man, so his reaction
should prove to be illuminating. I wonder if he'd
submit to an interview? Oops, someone is coming
in, time to play doorman.

Well, this should be interesting....

PAIGE STUDIED her reflection in the full-length mirror. Franco was right; the black skirt and matching
camisole did look better than the other outfits she'd
brought along with her tonight. The style and silky
fabric of the skirt made her feel sexy, too. Or maybe

that was an aftereffect of her afternoon at La Belle with Alex.

She'd never been so wanton before. So uninhibited. If Alex had that kind of effect on her just with his hands, imagine what he could do with the rest of his body! Paige had imagined it—too many times to count since Wednesday afternoon. And it had led her to only one conclusion.

She had to stop seeing him.

It wasn't even about trusting him anymore, it was about trusting herself. Despite everything she knew about Alex, his deception and his jail time, she still wanted him. Paige would have thought she'd have learned her lesson by now, but their erotic interlude at the spa had proved otherwise.

So she was abandoning her plan to wreak revenge on Alex. She simply wasn't willing to risk falling in love with him all over again. She'd have to find her answers another way. Going out with Nico tonight was a start. Though she intended to be honest with him about it.

If he wanted to back out of their date after she came clean about her former relationship with his brother, then so be it.

A knock at the door startled her from her reverie. She looked at the clock on the nightstand and saw that it was almost eight o'clock. She walked out of the bedroom, the faint aromas of Mongolian beef-and-almond chicken greeting her. One of her neighbors in the building must be cooking Chinese tonight.

As she opened the door, the rumble in her stomach told her she was hungry. The sight of Alex standing on the other side told her she was in big trouble.

She clenched the doorknob in her hand. "What are you doing here?"

He smiled as he held up two paper sacks. "Delivering dinner from the best Chinese restaurant in San Francisco. A little nourishment for my favorite college student." Then his gaze dropped to her outfit and desire flared in his eyes. "Do you always dress like this to study?"

Now was not a good time to chitchat. Nico could arrive at any moment.

"You have to go," she said, glancing behind him at the empty stairwell.

"But I just got here."

"I wasn't expecting you, Alex." It was time to make it clear to him that it was over. That there was no future between them. "I have...plans."

"Plans?" His gaze narrowed. "You mean a date?"

She swallowed. "Yes."

"With who?"

She didn't like his proprietary tone. "That's really none of your business."

"I say it is." He walked into her apartment without an invitation, setting the take-out sacks on the table before turning to face her. "Especially after La

Belle. I happen to love you, Paige. And I sure as hell don't want some stranger coming between us."

If he only knew. "No one can come between us, Alex, because there is no *us*."

He moved closer to her. "You can't deny we have something special, Paige. Something powerful."

"I'm not denying that you know how to seduce a woman. But what happened in that massage suite had nothing to do with love."

"I disagree." He moved closer to her and Paige's traitorous body tightened in response. "The connection between us is more than physical. That's why I fell in love with you last year when it was the last thing I wanted to do."

And that was the *last* thing she wanted to hear. But her retort died on her lips when she heard the sound of heavy footsteps on the stairs. She scrambled to think of some way to make Alex disappear. Could she hide him on the balcony? Have him slide down the rain gutter?

He cocked a brow as the sound of the footsteps ended right outside her apartment. "Shall I get the door for you?"

"It might be one of the other tenants," she said, dreading the inevitable.

It came anyway with a solid rap on the door. Sucking in a deep breath, she walked over and opened it. "Hello, Nico."

Alex muttered a curse behind her as his brother walked into the apartment. He carried a bottle of wine but seemed to forget about it when he spotted Alex.

"What are you doing here?" Nico inquired, setting the wine bottle on the table next to the take-out bags.

Alex clenched his jaw. "I was about to ask you the same question."

Paige stepped between them. "This is my fault." She turned to Nico. "I know your brother. In fact, I used to be engaged to him. I should have admitted as much when I came to your house the other day...."

"You were at my house?" Alex interjected.

"Mom won a contest," Nico informed him. "Free flowers for one month. Isn't that nice?"

Alex narrowed his gaze on him. "Cut the crap, Nico."

"Maybe you should just let me handle this, little brother."

"I don't think so." Alex made a grab for him, but Nico sidestepped out of his way.

"Stop it, please," Paige implored Alex. "Nico isn't to blame for any of this."

"Like hell," Alex growled.

The ring of the telephone broke the tension in the air. Grateful for a reprieve, Paige walked over to the end table to answer it.

"Hello?"

"It's me," Margo said, so softly that Paige could barely hear her.

"What's going on?" Her gaze flicked to the two men circling each other in the foyer of her apartment. Alex and Nico were so alike, yet so different. So why did the bad brother entice her more?

"Ed is here," Margo said, her voice still hushed.

Concern for her mother trumped the impending altercation in her apartment. She turned away from the men. "Mom, why are you whispering?"

"Because I don't want him to hear me."

Concern ebbed into panic. Maybe Ed Rooney did exist. Maybe he was some kind of crazed psychopath that her mother couldn't get out of the house.

"I'm coming home right now," Paige said.

"You'd better hurry," Margo warned her. "Before it's too late." Then she hung up the phone.

Or had it been disconnected? Paige stared at the receiver in her hand for a moment, then realized she had to find out.

Dropping the phone, she turned and lunged for her purse on the table. "I have to go."

"What about our date?" Nico asked.

"I'm sorry," she said, turning toward the door, her heart galloping in her chest. Was she really afraid for her mother or was she running away from the two of them?

She didn't have time to figure out the answer. Not when her mother might be in danger.

ALEX STARTED to follow her, but Nico grabbed his arm. "Not so fast. We need to come to an understanding."

Alex wrenched away from him, torn between catching up with Paige and punching his brother in the nose. "All you need to understand is that Paige Hanover is off-limits."

"I'm just trying to look out for you. The lady had you thrown into jail not too long ago. Remember that, Alex? And we still don't know for sure that she wasn't involved in the blackmail scheme."

"I know it," Alex countered, tired of his brother's head-of-the-family routine. It was time Alex made it clear that he was his own man, answering to no one. "She's not a threat to us."

"Then tell me why she showed up at the house with some phony story about our mother winning a contest. She asked to see her, Alex. What's that about?"

He didn't know the answer, but he could see the speculation in his brother's eyes. "You think she's got the tape? That she's going to blackmail Thea for more money?"

"It seems like the only logical explanation to me," Nico replied. "That's why I played along with her— to try and find out what she's thinking. I even fed her some bull about you being the black sheep of the Mackopoulos family."

"Thanks a lot!"

"Like I told you, she's snooping around for something. I'd just like to know what."

"And like I told you," Alex said between clenched teeth, "I'll handle Paige."

Nico snorted. "You're too crazy about her to see the obvious. How do you know she isn't looking for some dirt on you as payback for dumping her at the altar?"

"You know I didn't dump her," Alex retorted. "The judge charged me with contempt the day before our wedding. I realize now I should have come clean with Paige before then, but I didn't know that judge would throw me in jail."

Nico's anger faded. "And you still blame me, don't you? Because I was stupid enough to pay Weaver that twenty thousand dollars. That's why you couldn't testify, because you knew the secret about our father's affair would come out."

Alex sighed. "I never blamed you. Hell, I might have done the same thing in your place. You know I'd do anything to protect Thea."

His brother nodded. "So would I. That's why I'm not ready to trust Paige. I think it's possible she has the blackmail tape. The same tape that could destroy our mother. We need to find it before it appears one day and blows up in our faces."

Alex knew he was right. If that tape fell into the wrong hands, the year he'd spent in jail would have been for nothing. "Paige doesn't even know the tape exists, much less where to find it."

"Maybe," Nico conceded. "But I think one of us should make sure."

"Then I will." Alex spun out the door, determined to prove his brother wrong. He almost collided with the doorman hovering on the top step of the staircase.

"Leaving so soon?" Franco asked, stuffing a notepad and pen into his shirt pocket.

"Yes. Will you lock up the place when my brother leaves," Alex said. "I'm not sure when Paige is coming back."

Franco saluted him. "Will do—as soon as I ask him a few questions...."

Alex didn't stick around to find out what the doorman was babbling about. He needed to talk to Paige and judging by the bits and pieces he'd heard over the telephone, he knew just where to find her.

PAIGE RUSHED through the front door of her house, struggling to catch her breath. She held a can of Mace in one hand and her cell phone in the other. One sign of trouble and she'd spray first and ask questions later.

"Mom?"

"In here, dear," Margo called from the kitchen.

Her mother didn't sound frightened or even particularly concerned. Still, Paige entered the kitchen cautiously, not certain what she'd find there.

Margo sat at the kitchen table, sipping a cup of coffee, a plate of apple pie in front of her. Another slice of pie and a coffee cup sat in front of the empty chair across from her.

Paige set the cell phone and pepper spray on the counter, her throat growing tight as she realized the awful truth. There was no emergency. Because there was no Mr. Rooney.

"You look nice," Margo observed. "I love that skirt."

"Thanks," Paige said, her stomach tied up in knots. "Mom, we need to talk."

"I'm so glad you came over," Margo said, setting down her cup. "I wasn't expecting Ed tonight so I had to make that stealth phone call to let you know he was here. I know how much you've wanted to meet him."

"But he's not here," Paige said, ready to make her mother face the truth. "I'm afraid Ed Rooney only exists in your imagination."

Margo frowned up at her. "Have you been drinking?"

Paige wished she had. Right now she'd like nothing better than to be sitting in some cozy bar with Alex sipping a strawberry margarita. *No, not Alex,* she told herself firmly. And not strawberry. Anything but strawberry.

"Paige?" Margo asked, rising to her feet. "You look upset."

"Mom. I know it's been hard on you since Stanley disappeared. Maybe it's time you go talk to someone about it."

Margo shook her head. "I have no earthly idea what you are talking about."

"I'm talking about a psychotherapist," Paige said gently. "You've been imagining this man, Mr. Rooney, since that day you fainted in the store. Maybe the shock of seeing Alex suddenly appear out of nowhere had something to do with it. Especially when you'd convinced yourself that both he and Stanley had been abducted by aliens."

Margo started laughing. "You think Ed Rooney is a figment of my imagination?"

"What else can I think?" Paige replied. "Neither Alex nor I saw him in the store that day. Plus, you were sitting alone at The Drip on a supposed date with the man, just like you're doing now, with a coffee cup in front of an empty chair."

"It's all just a case of bad timing," Margo explained. "There's nothing crazy about it. I told you to hurry over here so you wouldn't miss him."

"I'm not saying you're crazy," Paige replied, trying to stay calm. "But look around you, Mom. There is no Mr. Rooney here."

"Well, of course not," Margo replied slowly, as if Paige were the one on the verge of a mental breakdown. "He's on the roof."

"The roof?" she echoed, fearing her mother was in the middle of a delusion. "What would he be doing on the roof?"

"Why don't we go ask him," Margo replied. "Then you can finally meet my mystery man and see for yourself that he's very real. As well as very handsome and quite intelligent."

Paige swallowed a sigh as she followed her mother out of the kitchen and toward the back door. She feared they wouldn't find anyone on the roof. That her mother was headed for a full-scale break-down.

But it was Paige who thought she was seeing things when she opened the door. Alex stood there, holding a stocky man in a hammerlock grip.

"Paige," Alex said, breathing hard, "meet Mr. Rooney."

10

"LET GO OF HIM," Margo cried, pulling Rooney away from Alex. The older man winced as he straightened to his full height, rubbing the back of his neck with one beefy hand.

"What's going on?" Paige asked as all of them moved into the kitchen.

"This maniac jumped me," Rooney complained. "That's what's going on. I'm lucky he didn't break my neck. I've got back problems, you know." He whirled on Alex. "Think about that before you tackle a guy next time!"

"I caught him skulking up the ladder to your roof," Alex said, ignoring Rooney's protests. "It looked to me like he was going to try and climb in one of the second-floor windows."

Margo shook her head. "You've got it all wrong. I gave permission for Ed to go up on the roof."

"Mother, tell me what is going on here?" Paige implored. "Why would Mr. Rooney want to go up on our roof?"

"I gave him access to the entire house," Margo replied. "He's looking for clues about Stanley."

Paige and Alex exchanged glances. Had her mother found another UFO buff to share her crazy theories?

"On the roof?" she said at last.

"You never know where you might find a vital clue." Rooney straightened his bow tie, shooting Alex a dirty look. "Now I think everybody should sit down and shut up for a minute so I can explain what's really going on here."

They grudgingly took his advice, pulling out chairs until all four of them were seated around the kitchen table.

"Now," Rooney began, "I don't know what Margo has told you about me, but I want to clear the air of any misunderstandings. My name is Ed Rooney and I work for *Myth Busters.*"

Paige frowned, more confused than ever. "The television show?"

Rooney nodded. "I never appear on camera, but I do all the fieldwork. My area of expertise is UFOs. The producers of the show hire me to debunk stories of alien sightings or abductions. Like the one about Stanley Weaver's unusual disappearance on *UFO Watch* the other night. I cut through all the mystique and they run the true version of the story to point out what really happened."

"You think you can find Weaver after all this time?" Alex asked, sounding skeptical. "The man disappeared without a trace."

"I have a few leads," Rooney conceded. "As well as some contacts in high places."

Paige looked at Alex, seeing the spark of interest in his eyes. It reaffirmed to her that he still wanted to find Stanley. That getting close to her had just been another gambit for information.

"So you've been using my mother," Paige said to Rooney, her voice rising with indignation for both of them. Were there no decent men left in the world? "Pretending you were interested in her when all you really wanted was the scoop about her relationship with Stanley."

"That's not fair, Paige," Margo interjected. "Ed told me everything tonight before you came over. He just needed to make sure my story was genuine and not something I made up for the show."

Paige looked at Rooney. "So you do believe her."

He hesitated. "I believe she believes it." He leaned forward. "Look, there's no such thing as alien abduction. I've cracked too many cases and proved them to be pure bunk for me to believe anything else."

"So now what?" Paige asked. "You go on the show and call my mother a liar?"

"I would never hurt Margo," Rooney said, casting a gaze at her mother that was more than businesslike.

Paige saw a blush rise to her mother's cheeks and she reconsidered her anger at Ed Rooney. Anyone who could make her mother forget about Stanley couldn't be all bad.

"What gives you the right to interfere in their lives this way?" Alex said with a scowl. "Just what do you think dragging Stanley Weaver back here will accomplish?"

Paige was confused by the question. Didn't Alex *want* to find Stanley? Or had that just been another lie? She still didn't know what *he* was doing here.

"Well, for one thing," Rooney replied, "it will put an end to this farce once and for all. Margo has been stuck in limbo thanks to this jerk. I, for one, will be happy to reveal whatever rock he's been hiding under she can finally get rid of him."

Paige turned to her mother. The same woman who only a week ago had talked about how important it was to stand by your man. "Get rid of him? Does that mean you've decided to divorce Stanley?"

"I haven't made any final decisions," Margo demurred, twisting her gold wedding band around her finger. "But you all seem to think Stanley ran out on me. I was there the night he disappeared. I heard the odd noises in the back yard. I saw the circles burned in the grass. Frankly, I welcome Ed's quest, if nothing else than to prove to everyone that I've been right all along."

Rooney stared at her. "I won't give up until I find him, Margo. I'll be on this story day and night."

She smiled at him. "That sounds promising."

Paige gaped at the two of them. A UFO buff and a

UFO debunker, making goo-goo eyes at each other in her kitchen. What better way to prove that opposites really do attract?

Alex seemed oblivious to the romance blooming in front of his eyes. He turned toward Rooney. "What leads do you have on Weaver so far? Or is that top secret?"

"Hell, no," Rooney replied. "My job is about revealing secrets, not keeping them."

"That's refreshing," Paige murmured.

Alex ignored the barb. "So tell us what you know?"

"Stanley Weaver is your standard scam artist. His real name is Wally Stanislawski, although he goes by several aliases. He specializes in romancing wealthy widows, then relieving them of every dime they've got. Usually through some fake real estate deal or phony business investment. I know of at least two outstanding warrants for his arrest."

"So I take it he's pulled this kind of disappearing act before?"

Rooney nodded. "He's always manages to stay one step ahead of the law, usually lying low for a year or two before targeting his next victim."

"But where does he lie low?"

"That's the question no one can seem to answer," Rooney replied. "He's got a sister, Hildegard Stanislawski, who grew up with him in Southern California, but so far I haven't traced her. She's probably married and living under her husband's name."

"So do you think this sister would know where to find Stanley?" Paige asked.

Rooney shrugged. "Maybe. Another possibility is that one of his loyal ex-wives is hiding him somewhere. I'm scheduled to interview one of them tomorrow across the Bay in Orinda."

"I don't understand why Stanley picked me," Margo said, still perplexed by the revelations about her missing husband. "I'm not wealthy."

Rooney sighed. "I haven't figured that one out yet. It doesn't fit his usual MO. The whirlwind courtship fits, but he stayed in the marriage for almost a year. Normally, Weaver courts a woman, marries her, then cleans out her bank account within three months before moving on to his next victim. He's already wanted in three states for forgery, grand theft and...bigamy."

"Bigamy?" Margo gasped. "You mean he's been married to more than one woman at a time?"

Ed met her gaze. "I mean he's still married to many of them right now."

They all stared at him as the meaning of his words sank in. Then Margo collapsed onto the table in a dead faint.

They all rushed over to her at once, the men gently laying her on the kitchen carpet as Paige wet a washcloth under the sink, then wrung it out before placing it on her forehead.

"She'll be all right," Paige told a worried Ed. "This is how Mom deals with shock."

"I should have broken the news more gently," he said ruefully. "Eased her into it."

Paige picked up her mother's hand and rubbed it between her own. "I don't think there's any way to ease into the news that your husband has other wives scattered across the country." She looked up at him. "How many wives does he have?"

"Four that I know of," Rooney replied. "Five others have already divorced him, but there are still some who are waiting for him to come back. Who won't believe the man they loved betrayed them."

Paige looked at Alex and found him staring at her. She quickly glanced away before he could see the pain in her eyes. She'd done the exact same thing as those deluded women, waiting for a whole year before deciding to move on with her life. Only her man had come back to her. She just didn't know what to do with him now.

Margo's eyelids began to flutter, her chest rising as she sucked in a deep breath.

"We can't just leave her here on the floor," Rooney said, his face etched with worry.

"I'll carry her to the sofa," Alex offered, bending down to pick her up in his arms.

"No, I'll do it," Rooney said, trying to move him out of the way.

But Alex didn't budge, scooping Margo up like she weighed no more than a feather. "You have a bad back, remember?"

They followed him into the living room, where he

gently laid Margo on the sofa. She was starting to come around now, her eyes fluttering open and fixing on Ed Rooney.

Ed perched on the edge of the sofa beside her, taking her hands in his own.

"Looks like Ed can handle it from here," Alex said, his voice low enough for only Paige to hear. "I need to talk to you. Alone."

"Now?"

He nodded. "Meet me on the roof."

"WHAT'S THIS ALL ABOUT?" Paige asked as they stood on the rooftop, the warm night breeze rustling through the wild prairie grass planted in pots around them. She didn't like being up here alone with Alex. It made her feel too vulnerable.

He stared out into the night sky, his shoulders tense. "I'm not sure how to tell you this, Paige."

"Tell me what?" she asked warily, preparing herself for the worst. "Something as shocking as what Rooney just told my mother. Something like...the truth."

He turned to face her. "Yes."

She stared up at him, confusion, frustration and desire pooling inside of her until she finally lashed out. "You've lied to me since the beginning, Alex. You're still keeping something from me. Why? To protect me or protect yourself?"

"Both, I guess." A muscle flexed in his jaw. "But it's about to blow up in my face, thanks to Rooney."

"Rooney?" His answer defused her anger. "What does he have to do with us?"

Alex met her gaze, his eyes almost black in the moonlight. "You told me there is no us."

"You know what I mean," she replied, trying to ignore the wave of warmth washing through her when he looked at her that way, reminding her of their interlude at the spa. But she needed to focus on the present. "Just say it, Alex. I'm tired of playing games."

He gave a brisk nod, ready to get down to business. "I know how Stanley Weaver was scamming your mother. How he was scamming both of you."

Dread settled low in her stomach. Something niggled at her, something she hadn't put together yet. "How?"

"He was blackmailing your clients at Bay Bouquets. The business executives that contracted for service and maintenance of the office plants you provided them."

A long moment passed while Paige absorbed his words. Stanley had gone out on most of the service calls in various offices. But how could that lead to blackmail?

Alex anticipated her question. "Weaver bugged the plants with a recording device. Then when he came across sensitive information, usually of a personal nature, he offered the tapes in exchange for money. A lot of money."

She sank down onto a stone bench, trying to process what he'd just told her. "Stanley Weaver was shaking down my customers?"

"Yes." Alex sat down next to her. "He wasn't cheap, either. He hit my father up for twenty thousand dollars."

Paige looked up at him, feeling sick inside. "He blackmailed your father?"

Alex nodded. "My dad never knew about it. He was gravely ill when the first demand for money arrived. My brother and I ignored the threats at first, but as they became more and more frequent, we were afraid that our mother would come across one of them. She was dealing with the stress of my father's illness and didn't need anything else to worry about. So Nico paid it, hoping that would be the end of it."

The implications of what he'd just told her began to sink in. "How could I have let this happen?"

"It's not your fault," Alex assured her, reaching for her hand, then pulling back. "You trusted him. Just like you trusted me."

She thought about some of her longtime customers who had abruptly quit doing business with her. Had they been Stanley's victims, too? How much damage did he do? "You should have told me from the beginning. I might have been able to do something about it."

Alex met her gaze. "I couldn't be sure you weren't in on it," he said bluntly. "Not until I got to know you."

The rest of the pieces of this puzzle began to snap into place. "So you were investigating more than Stanley last year when we began dating. You were suspicious of me, too."

He nodded. "I thought it was possible that you and Stanley and Margo might all be in on this together. When he disappeared with our twenty thousand dollars without turning over a tape, I thought there might be an off chance that you or Margo had it in your possession."

"What exactly was on that tape?"

"Something highly personal to my family," Alex said after a long moment.

"So you still don't trust me," she said softly.

"Do you trust me?" he rejoined.

It was a loaded question, because Paige had trusted him enough to come apart in his arms. Just like she'd trusted him to stop when she'd asked him to. But could she trust him not to break her heart again? "I don't know what to think anymore."

First, Rooney broke the bombshell about her stepfather's bigamy, then Alex was telling her that Stanley Weaver was a blackmailer as well. She and Margo had turned picking the wrong men into an art form.

"Why did you bring me up here to tell me all this?" she asked suddenly, sensing there was something more. "Why now?"

His face darkened. "Because I want you to stay away from Nico while I'm gone."

She blanched at the sudden change of subject. Paige had forgotten all about Nico. "Where are you going?"

"To find Stanley Weaver before Rooney does."

"Why?" she asked him. "Rooney's the expert in searching for missing persons. He can track Stanley down and put him in jail where he belongs."

"Because Stanley still has our twenty thousand dollars and the master tape. I want to destroy that tape before Rooney finds it or else it could end up on *Myth Busters*."

"He might have made copies."

"Then I'll look for those, too," Alex said, setting his jaw. "I won't let Stanley Weaver destroy my family. He's destroyed too much already."

Paige knew he was talking about their broken engagement. But Stanley had brought them together, not torn them apart. Alex was responsible for that because he'd put his loyalty to his family above his loyalty to her. But she couldn't blame him for that, no matter how much it hurt her.

His hands curled over the side of the concrete bench. "So do you promise to stay away from Nico while I'm gone?"

"I don't have to promise," she replied. "Because I'm coming with you."

He shook his head. "No way."

She stood up, ready to do battle. Alex brought out the warrior woman in her. Only she'd been waging battle against him. Now it was time to join forces.

"We'll have better luck catching Stanley if there are two of us," Paige said, arguing her case. "Besides, I know Stanley and you don't. I know his habits and his hobbies." Then she dropped her bombshell. "And I think I know where to find him."

He gaped at her. "You do?"

She nodded. "When Rooney was talking about his sister, the name Hildegard struck a chord with me. A couple of months ago, I was cleaning out my mother's house so she could sell it. That included everything that Stanley had left behind. His clothes, books, movies."

"And you found information about his sister?"

"Maybe." She hoped it wasn't just wishful thinking. "There were a bunch of tourist brochures in a desk drawer. I didn't think anything of it at the time because Stanley was always talking about taking my mom on an exotic vacation somewhere. Talking, but never going. He had brochures for Tahiti, Rio and New Zealand. And one for a bed-and-breakfast in the tiny town of Redwing, California."

"How does that connect to his sister?"

"The name of the bed-and-breakfast was Hildy's Hideaway."

Alex gave a slow nod. "That sounds like a good place to start looking for good old Stanley."

"So, are you driving, or am I?" When he started to protest, she held up one hand to forestall him. "I'm going and that's final. Stanley used my mother and he used me. I'm not going to let him get away with it. Besides, you need me."

He moved closer to her and Paige's breath hitched in her throat. "I've been trying to tell you that since I came back."

She swallowed hard at the raw desire she saw reflected in his eyes. "Then let me come with you. Stanley almost destroyed my mother and he could still destroy my business. I can't just idly sit by and let that happen."

Alex still didn't look convinced. "It might be dangerous. I don't want you to get hurt."

"I've already been hurt because of this mess," she replied, lifting her chin. "I'm not going to play the victim anymore. You're taking me with you. End of discussion."

His nostrils flared. "Do you know what you're asking?"

"It seems simple enough to me."

"Nothing has ever been simple between us." Then Alex grabbed her and kissed her. His mouth clung to hers, primal and hot, with none of the gentleness he'd shown her that day at the spa.

A flash of heat lightning shot through her as she kissed him back, her tongue battling with his for control even as her brain told her to back away. But her body wasn't listening as she sank into him, the feel of his hard length making her weak with need.

At last, he broke away from her, his breathing heavy. "If you come with me, we'll be spending day and night together. And I'll do my damnedest to make you forget all about Nico or any other man. Except me."

Then he stalked toward the ladder without a backward glance. "Be ready first thing in the morning. We're leaving for Redwing at nine o'clock sharp."

Paige watched him descend until he disappeared. Then she raised her fingers to her lips, still tender from the intensity of his branding kiss.

Day and night. Something told her this would be a trip she'd never forget.

11

Franco's Notes:

ALL HELL BROKE LOOSE here tonight after Paige left. No fights, unfortunately, but it still made for good drama. Two brothers in love with the same woman! Perhaps I should introduce a love triangle into my story. Then again, why stop there? I could make it a quadrangle. Or even a sextet. The possibilities are endless....

PAIGE RETURNED to the apartment that night to give Margo and Ed some privacy and to give herself time alone to think. She'd only been gone a little over an hour, but her entire life had been turned upside down. Her mother was falling in love and now she and Alex were going after Stanley.

Her head was still swimming with everything she'd learned tonight about the con artist her mother had married. It almost made the things Alex had done seem minor in comparison. *Almost.* She knew he wanted her. She was even fairly certain now that he loved her. But he didn't trust *her* enough to tell her how Stanley had blackmailed his family. Which made her wonder, all over again, if she could trust *him*.

She walked inside the apartment building, carrying the suitcase she'd packed earlier to take on her trip to Redwing. A weekend getaway, she'd told her mother, not wanting her to worry. At the moment, Paige was doing enough worrying for both of them.

"Oh, goody, you're back," Franco exclaimed, turning away from his television set as she walked inside the foyer. "I'm dying to know if you're going to pick bachelor number one or bachelor number two."

"I don't know what I'm going to do," she replied honestly.

"You look beat," Franco observed, then patted the chair he'd just vacated. "Here, sit down and tell me all about it."

She barely knew the man, but Paige had to talk to someone or she'd go mad. Setting down her suitcase, she settled into the chair. "It's a long story."

"My favorite kind," Franco replied, pulling out a pad and pencil.

She arched a brow. "You're taking notes?"

"Just so I can keep up. I've got a lousy memory."

She started at the beginning, leaving out only those private moments at the spa. There were some things Franco didn't need to know.

"With Alex I just wanted revenge," she concluded. "He had burned me and I wanted to burn him back."

Franco nodded sagely. "Revenge is good. After Marlon broke up with me, I replaced his collection of Billie Holiday CDs with Alvin and the Chipmunks. Juvenile, I know, but extremely satisfying."

"Alex didn't just break up with me," Paige told him. "He left me at the altar."

Franco winced. "Ouch."

"But now I know there were extenuating circumstances," she explained, finding herself making excuses for him. "Very complicated extenuating circumstances. Yet, that still doesn't change the fact that he lied to me. If he did it once, he could do it again. I'm not sure I'm willing to take that kind of risk."

"Then it sounds to me like you should pick bachelor number two."

"Nico?" She shook her head. "He seems nice enough, but he's not really my type. He's not..."

"Alex?" Franco finished for her.

"Exactly." Paige sighed. "I should probably forget about both of them."

"That is another option," Franco agreed. "Love is a tempting buffet. You just have to choose the right dish or you'll get heartburn." Then his eyes lit up. "Ooh, that was good. I have to write that down."

"How is your screenplay coming along?"

"I think it's going to be fabulous as soon as I can pull all the pieces together," Franco replied. "But

fate is definitely smiling on me because I found a diamond ring in the street gutter yesterday and
hocked it for enough money to buy a new laptop
computer!"

Her engagement ring. The one she'd thrown over
the balcony right before Alex had shown up in her
life again. Maybe Franco was right—it was a sign. A
sign that she and Alex weren't meant to be together.

"Congratulations," she told him, rising out of the
chair and reaching for her suitcase. It had been a
long, tumultuous day and she was too drained to
make any major decisions about her life right now.
"I hope your screenplay is a big hit."

His eyes flicked to her skirt. "I'm sure it will be."

"Thank you for letting me borrow this again tonight," she said, smoothing one hand over her hip.
"I'm afraid it was wasted though, since I didn't
have a date after all."

"Well, there's still the weekend," Franco said.
"Maybe you should take the skirt and go out to hunt
down bachelors number three, four and five. Add a
few more dishes to the buffet before you make your
selection."

She laughed at his analogy. "I'm going away for
the weekend, so the buffet will have to wait."

"Bummer." Franco arched a brow. "Unless
you're going away with a man?"

"I'm going with Alex to a bed-and-breakfast up
north, but it's not a romantic getaway."

"You'll still want to look good," he said. "Take

the skirt with you, then give me all the juicy details when you get back.''

"Are you sure?''

"I absolutely insist,'' Franco said. ''Now, do you want me to carry that suitcase upstairs for you.'' He checked his watch. ''*UFO Watch* doesn't come on for five minutes, so I have a little time.''

"I can handle it,'' she assured him, starting up the steps. ''Thanks for listening, Franco.''

"Anytime,'' he said, waving to her. ''Anytime at all.''

When she reached her apartment, she was surprised to find the door unlocked. And even more surprised to find Nico still inside.

"Hope you don't mind that I decided to stick around,'' he said, rising from the sofa. ''I'd still like to have dinner with you tonight, if you're up to it.''

Nico Mackopoulos might be a dish, but she knew, at that moment, that he didn't belong in her buffet. ''I'm sorry, Nico, but I don't think that's a good idea.''

He smiled. ''I see my brother has scared you away from me.''

"It's not that,'' she said truthfully, though Alex had made his feelings very clear. ''I should have never agreed to date you in the first place.''

He nodded. ''I think I understand.''

She was glad one of them did. Setting her suitcase down, she rubbed one hand over the back of her neck, trying to release the knot of tension there.

"At least join me in a glass of wine," Nico said, picking up the bottle he'd brought over.

She owed him at least that much. "I'd love a glass of wine. Let me find a corkscrew."

He followed her into the kitchen. "You left here in quite a hurry. Is everything all right?"

"Yes," she hedged, handing him the corkscrew. "I thought my mother was in trouble, but it was a simple misunderstanding."

He popped open the bottle while she retrieved two wineglasses from the cupboard. It occurred to her that Nico seemed to be taking all this very well for a man who didn't know she'd been engaged to his brother until an hour ago.

Or did he?

Nico poured them each a glass of the dark red merlot while she mentally pulled some of the pieces of this puzzle together.

"You knew about Alex and I, didn't you?" Paige asked, as she took her glass from him. "Even before that day I came to your house."

He took a sip of his wine. "Yes, I did."

"But you played along anyway."

"I had my reasons."

It suddenly became clear to her. "Did you think I'd bugged the flowers I brought to your home? That I was in on Stanley Weaver's extortion scheme?"

He blanched. "Alex told you about that?"

"Yes, and I can assure you that it came as a complete surprise."

"Of course, I only have your word on that," Nico said. "Though the flowers were clean. I checked."

"And if they hadn't been clean?" she inquired, knowing both Nico and Alex had reason to be suspicious of her but hating it anyway. "Then what?"

"Fortunately, that isn't the case."

Maybe she didn't want to know the answer. Paige took another sip of her wine, wondering how long Nico planned to stay. She was emotionally drained and had a long weekend ahead of her. *A weekend with Alex.*

"I do want to set the record straight before I go," Nico said, setting his glass on the coffee table. "I'm also the one who sent you that e-mail proposal last year, signing Alex's name. I thought it might make you open up to him. Needless to say, he wasn't too happy with me."

"Alex had told me someone else sent that e-mail proposal, but he didn't say it was his own brother."

Nico nodded. "Family loyalty comes before everything else for a Mackopoulos. You'd do well to remember that."

It almost sounded like a warning. One she didn't need because she'd already seen evidence of it. Alex had chosen protecting his family over her last year. There was no reason to believe anything had changed.

His eyes flicked to her skirt. "Although, there's

something about you, Paige. I can't quite put my finger on it, but I think I'm beginning to understand why my brother acted like a rabid dog when I showed up at your door tonight."

He drained the last of his wine, then stood up. "I'd better go."

Nico Mackopoulos hadn't exactly given them his blessing, but he seemed to believe that his brother loved her. Still, the truth was that she'd never have definitive proof of Alex's feelings for her. She'd have to go on faith, just like she had last year. Just like her mother had with Stanley. Was it worth the risk?

There was only one way to find out.

IT RAINED all the way to Redwing. She and Alex talked about the weather. The budding romance of Margo and Ed. The odds of the Giants winning the pennant. As if by unspoken agreement, they pushed their personal problems away for the five-hour trip and just enjoyed each other's company.

But as they pulled into the small town of four thousand people, the reason for the drive came rushing back to Paige. They were here to track down Stanley Weaver, aka Wally Stanislawski, each for their own reason. She wanted to put an end to the chaos her stepfather had caused in their lives. Alex wanted the tape that still threatened his family.

And when they both got what they wanted—then what?

Neither one of them had broached that subject to-day, either.

"The bed-and-breakfast should be right down this road," Alex said, checking the map they'd picked up at a gas station earlier.

"There it is." Paige pointed to a large white house with a sign posted in a yard. The green lawn was bordered by purple lilac bushes. "Hildy's Hide-away."

Alex pulled his car into the circular drive and parked near the sidewalk. Then he looked at Paige. "Are you sure you want to be involved in this?"

"It's a little late to back out now," she replied, though her stomach kept twisting into nervous knots. But was she more anxious about finding Stanley or about spending time alone with Alex?

"Then let's go," he said, climbing out of the car. They unloaded their suitcases from the trunk, then walked up the wide stoop that led to the front door.

A cheerful bell tinkled as they walked inside. The living room looked as if it were straight out of a Norman Rockwell painting with a rustic hardwood floor covered with a tapestry rug and filled with vintage furniture. Intricately carved moldings adorned the ten-foot ceiling; no cobwebs in sight. The room was immaculate and so was the woman who suddenly appeared in the arched doorway.

Close to sixty with snow-white hair and an easy smile, the proprietress of Hildy's Hideaway had twinkling green eyes with laugh lines etched deep in the corners. Paige couldn't help but notice the striking resemblance to Stanley in the widow's peak and slight overbite.

"Hello, I'm Hildy," she said, walking toward the antique desk in front of them. "You must be the Macks."

Paige opened her mouth to correct the woman, then closed it again. Alex had made the reservations. He'd obviously decided to resurrect his old alias.

"That's right," he confirmed. "I'm Alex and this is my wife, Paige."

She skittered a glance at her make-believe husband, wondering when he'd dreamed this story up.

"Welcome to Redwing," Hildy said, pushing the guest book toward them. "I have your room all ready for you."

"Great," Alex said, handing the pen to Paige.

She leaned over to sign the guest book, her gaze quickly scanning the other names. She didn't see a Stanley Weaver or a Wally Stanislawski listed anywhere.

Not that she'd expected it to be this easy. Although, Hildy's resemblance to Stanley couldn't be denied. Right down to the same benign green eyes.

Focusing once again on the task in front of her, Paige carefully signed the guest book as Mr. and Mrs. Mack.

"You're in room four," Hildy announced. "That's at the top of the stairs, then take a left. That's one of the honeymoon suites, so it has its own private bath."

The honeymoon suite? Paige looked at Alex, but he'd already picked up their suitcases and was heading toward the stairs.

"Oh, Mrs. Mack," Hildy called behind her.

It took Paige a moment to realize the woman was referring to her. "Yes?" she replied, turning around.

"Here's a little something I like to give to all my honeymoon couples."

She handed her a small gift basket filled with fresh fruit, home-baked cookies and a small bottle of champagne. "I wish you two every happiness."

"Thank you," Paige said, returning the woman's smile. Part of her hoped that Stanley hadn't dragged this kind woman in on his illegal schemes. Even if it did mean Redwing was a dead end. "This is lovely."

"Let me know if you need anything," Hildy said as Paige started up the stairs.

Alex was already in the room when she got there.

"Aren't you going to carry me over the threshold?" Paige asked.

He started toward her, but she walked through the door before he could reach her. "I was just kidding. But why in the world did you tell her we're on our honeymoon?"

"Because I thought it would be a good cover for us," Alex said. "Besides, this was the only room that was available, so I figured we should make the most of it."

Make the most of it? She looked at the double bed. "And where will you be sleeping?"

"Wherever you want me to." He moved closer, taking the basket out of her hands at the same time he leaned down to kiss her.

Caught by surprise, she parted her lips and he took advantage of the situation by easing his tongue into her mouth. Heat rolled through her as she let him pull her closer. He deepened the kiss, setting off a maelstrom of emotions inside her. She considered this weekend a test of her willpower and he was already pushing her to the limit.

At last he broke the kiss, though his mouth still lingered close to hers. "Wherever you want me, Paige," he said huskily. "Whenever you want me."

12

THE IMPLICIT PROMISE in his words sent a delicious tingle through her body. But Paige didn't know what she wanted yet. And until she figured it out, she wasn't going to make any decisions she might regret later.

"You can sleep in the window seat," she said, pointing to the bay window.

He followed the direction of her finger. "That window seat looks to be about six feet long. I'm six foot three. I don't think I'm going to fit."

"Then I'll sleep in the window seat," she replied, not wanting to get into a debate about their sleeping arrangements. A debate she could too easily lose to the temptations he freely offered.

"Forget it," Alex said, playing the gentleman now. "You take the bed. I'll just sleep on the floor."

"A wood floor?" She shook her head. "I don't think so. The window seat looks perfectly comfortable to me. It will be a new experience."

"I'm all for new experiences." He looked at her in a way that made a hot blush rise to her cheeks.

"Then it's settled," she said, grabbing a cookie

from the basket before sitting down on the edge of the bed. "Now, we need to come up with a plan to catch Stanley."

"The first thing we need to determine is if Hildy is Stanley's sister," Alex said.

"She is," Paige affirmed. "I'm almost sure of it. They share the same distinctive facial features and I remember him telling my mother once that his sister was a great cook." She licked the crumbs off her fingers. "Just wait until you taste these cookies. They're incredible."

He grabbed one out of the basket. "We could still use some solid evidence. Maybe I'll snoop around the place after everyone is in bed for the night. See what I can find out."

She scowled at him. "That is the dumbest idea I've ever heard."

"Why?"

"Because if you're caught and the police discover that you have a record, they'll throw you right back in jail."

He stared at her and Paige realized too late that she'd spilled one of the secrets he hadn't told her yet. One he probably had never planned to tell her.

Alex set down his cookie. "What makes you think I have a record?"

It was too late to backpedal now. Besides, she wanted everything out in the open between them. No more lies. No more secrets. "Because when I called to drop the charges against you the Monday after I had you arrested, the desk sergeant told me you had recently been released from jail."

"Did he tell you why I was in jail?"

She shook her head. "No, and neither did Nico."

"Nico?" His eyes narrowed. "You asked my brother about it?"

"He brought the subject up when I delivered the flowers to your mother's house. But Nico didn't tell me why you were in jail because, in his words, he didn't want to air the family's dirty laundry."

"Great," Alex said, muttering a colorful curse under his breath. "My brother and his big mouth."

"So you never planned to tell me," she asked, disappointed by his reaction.

"It's not exactly something I'm proud of."

"Don't you think I know that?" she asked softly. "Why were you in jail, Alex?"

He hesitated and for a moment Paige thought he wasn't going to tell her. That he didn't want to trust her with the truth. Or was he afraid of her reaction to it?

"I was jailed for contempt of court," he said at last. "I refused to testify in a grand-jury trial."

"But why?"

His jaw tightened. "Because they were trying to build a case against Mackopoulos Imports for misusing company funds. As the financial manager, I was privy to all the business transactions and they were legitimate. As Nico's brother, I knew he'd illegitimately borrowed twenty thousand dollars from the company's coffers because he was desperate. Though he did eventually pay the money back."

Paige closed her eyes as the last bite of cookie turned to dust in her mouth. Her stepfather had caused this. He'd blackmailed a sick man for twenty thousand dollars and, in doing so, he'd indirectly sent Alex to jail.

"That's the reason I disappeared last year, Paige," Alex explained, his voice tight. "I knew I was scheduled to testify in court the week we were to be married, but I didn't think the judge would throw me in jail."

"You could have called me," she said, remembering the awful devastation she'd felt at thinking he'd just walked out on her. "You could have let me help you."

"There was absolutely nothing you could have done and I wasn't about to drag you into that mess. I didn't want you to get hurt."

"But I was hurt," she said, her voice a whisper now. "More than you'll ever know."

He met her gaze, her pain reflected in his eyes. "I know now I should have trusted you. That year was hell for me, too, Paige. I knew you'd end up hating me. And I was right."

"I don't hate you," she breathed. "Believe me, I've tried, Alex. But I can't seem to hate you."

"Then I guess the question is," he said softly, "if you can ever love me again."

He was asking too much, too soon. Or was he?

She was tired of constantly looking over her shoulder, nursing the wounds of the past, regretting the mistakes they'd both made.

It was time to move forward. And they could only do that by putting the past completely behind them.

She brushed the cookie crumbs off her lap and stood up. "I think we should start our search for Stanley."

He started to say something, then just gave a brisk nod. "All right, what do you have in mind?"

"I brought a photograph of him along with me," she said, reaching into her bag to show him. "I thought we could pass it around to some local businesspeople. Maybe they've seen him."

"What if word gets back to Hildy?"

She shrugged. "If that happens, we'll just tell her the truth, or at least part of it. That Stanley is married to my mother and that he disappeared several months ago. We're not cops. She won't have any reason to suspect we're on to him."

"Maybe," Alex allowed. "In the meantime, I think circulating that picture is a good idea. We might even try it out on some of the neighbors. See if they've seen Stanley skulking around here."

"Skulking?" she said with a smile. "That's an interesting word."

"I did a lot of reading while I was in jail," he said lightly. "It really improved my vocabulary."

"I'm impressed."

He headed toward the door, holding it open for

her. "Do you want to know what tonight's vocabulary word is?"

Paige slipped the picture back into her purse, then slung the strap over her shoulder. "I can't wait to hear it."

His gaze slid toward the bed, then back to her again. "Anticipation."

ALEX HAD BLISTERS by the time they finished flashing Stanley Weaver's picture up and down the main thoroughfare of Redwing. Even more frustrating, nobody recognized him. The name didn't ring any bells, either. Nor did the name Wally Stanislawski.

The only high point of the day was stopping for dinner at a local diner. The food was all home-cooked and they stuffed themselves on pot roast with gravy and glazed vegetables, sharing a slice of strawberry pie for dessert.

The strawberries reminded him of that day at the spa and judging by the fiery blush on Paige's cheeks when he fed her a bite, she remembered it as well.

Good. He didn't want to be the only one half-crazed with lust. She might not be able to admit she loved him, but even she couldn't deny she desired him. It was evident in the way she'd kissed him today. The way she stared at him when she thought he wasn't looking.

Now he just had to figure out what to do about it. He'd tried the subtle approach as well as the direct approach. Neither one had been successful. Which left him with only one other option.

He had to wait for her to come to him.

By the time they returned to Hildy's Hideaway and settled in for the night, it was obvious that she was in no hurry to do anything but go to sleep.

"Here we go," Paige said, lifting the lid of the window seat to reveal a storage compartment underneath. "All the blankets we could ever need to keep warm."

He wasn't having any problem staying warm. The woman damn near gave him a fever. Especially while wearing that long silk nightgown that draped over her lush curves in a way that made him ache to see what was underneath.

Paige arranged the blankets and pillows on the cushion of the window seat, then settled in for the night. "This is perfect."

"It seems silly not to make use of a double bed," Alex observed. He lay with his shoulders propped up against the feather down pillows, his arms folded behind his head.

"I'll be fine," she said, avoiding his gaze. "Though I'm a little worried that you'll be cold without a shirt on."

"Cold is not my problem," he said wryly. Then he leaned over to turn off the light. "Good night, Paige."

"Good night, Alex."

He lay in the darkness, listening to the silence. It

was too quiet in this town. How could he possibly get up and sneak around the house without someone hearing him? Maybe Paige was right. It was a bad idea.

He turned onto his side, now able to hear Paige's soft, somnolent breathing. He couldn't believe she could fall asleep so easily. Then again, she wasn't so aroused that she was about to bust out of her skin.

Maybe he needed another cold shower. Alex flung back the quilt, ready to take refuge under a stream of icy water that was becoming all too familiar. Then he hesitated. The sound of the shower running would wake her up. She'd want to know what was wrong with him, then figure it out anyway no matter what excuse he made up.

Then he'd see the guilt and uncertainty in her eyes, just like he did every time he kissed her. Guilt because she wanted him as much as he wanted her. Uncertainty because she didn't know if she could trust her own feelings.

Thanks to him.

"Hell," he muttered to himself, climbing back into bed. He didn't want to put her through that again. Alex had made his feelings perfectly clear to her tonight. Now it was up to Paige to act on them.

Or not.

It was the "or not" part that was driving him crazy. He forced his eyes closed, trying to think of anything besides the passionate woman he loved sleeping only a few feet away from him. Counting sheep didn't work. Neither did reciting the multiplication tables. Then his mind began to drift to that day at the spa. The shape of her breasts. The dusky pink color of her nipples. The sweet cry of her release.

Hardly thoughts to lull him to sleep. Just the opposite, in fact. After a restless thirty minutes, he finally got out of bed and padded silently over to the window seat. The full moon cast an ethereal glow over Paige's face. She was so beautiful, it made his throat ache just to look at her.

He bent down and lightly kissed her brow. A soft sigh escaped her lips and he smiled to himself at the sound. Then he turned around and went back to his bed.

Despite the throbbing ache in his groin, he told himself he'd wait as long as it took for her to come to him. Either here or back in San Francisco.

Because Paige was worth it.

THE NEXT MORNING, Paige and Alex sat in the sunny dining room of Hildy's Hideaway and enjoyed a farm-style breakfast. The place was full of couples of all ages, each pair seated at a small round table adorned with a vase of daisies and a morning newspaper.

"This place is great," Alex said, picking up a glass of orange juice. "But I think we've hit a dead end. Stanley's not here."

Paige hid a yawn behind her hand, not wanting to

admit that she hadn't slept all that well on the window seat last night. "We can still try talking to Hildy. Maybe she knows where to find Stanley."

"If she does, it's not likely she'll tell us. Unless we can come up with a nonthreatening reason for trying to find him. Hildy's bound to be skittish, given her brother's checkered past."

But she barely heard him, she was too focused on the way his mouth moved. Paige had been staring at him a lot lately. Even waking up early this morning so she could study him while he slept.

Letting herself look her fill at the face she'd tried so hard to hate.

She found herself memorizing the line of his jaw, the shape of his firm lips, the thickness of the lashes fanning his cheeks. Barely resisting the urge to reach out and stroke the dark shadow of whiskers there. To run her fingers through his thick, dark hair.

So what was stopping her? Other than her own fears of history repeating itself. But even that wasn't much of a factor anymore, now that she knew Alex had left her against his will last year, going to jail instead of to their wedding.

"Well?" he asked, his fork poised above his plate, golden syrup dripping off a chunk of his buttermilk pancake. "Any ideas?"

It took her a moment to realize he was talking about finding Stanley. "I say we should just come right out and ask Hildy about her brother. She might surprise us by telling the truth."

"That truth might be that she doesn't know where he is."

"I know." She reached for a blueberry muffin, splitting it in half. "But that might not be all bad."

He looked up at her in surprise, chewing thoughtfully on his pancake. "What do you mean?"

"If Ed Rooney has proof that Stanley or Wally, or whatever his name is, was married to my mother while he was still wed to other women, then that marriage can probably be annulled whether we find Stanley or not."

"But that only solves one problem," Alex said. "The possibility still exists that Stanley could come back wanting more money from the people he blackmailed before. The tape he made of my father is still out there."

"You could always go to the police."

Alex shook his head. "Nico and I made a pact never to let that tape become public. Which is exactly what might happen if the case went to trial."

"So you'd pay Stanley more money just to keep that secret?"

He stared at her for a long moment. "Family comes first for a Mackopoulos."

Nico had told her the same thing. It seemed obvious to her that they were protecting their mother. What else would inspire this kind of loyalty?

Then she looked up and saw something that made her forget everything else. "I don't believe it."

"It's true," Alex retorted, under the mistaken impression that she was contradicting him.

Paige grabbed the newspaper lying on the table and held it in front of her face. "Stanley just walked into the dining room."

"Where?" Alex asked, turning around.

"Don't look!" she exclaimed in a harsh whisper. "I don't want him to see me. He'll get spooked and run."

Alex turned back to her. "Are you sure it's Stanley? That doesn't look like the same man in those pictures."

"I'm positive," she replied. "He's changed the color of his hair and he's wearing bifocals now, but it's still Stanley."

"What's he doing?" Alex asked, his back now to the man.

"Walking to a table near the window. He's sitting down now," Paige reported, "And Hildy just walked in with a plate of bacon and eggs. Looks like he's a regular here."

"Damn," Alex muttered under his breath, "I wanted her to be one of the good guys."

"Me, too."

"Has Stanley seen you?" Alex asked. "Did he recognize you?

She shook her head, her face still partially concealed by the newspaper. "I don't think so. He's oblivious to everyone in here except his sister. Now she's bringing him a cup of coffee."

"Does she look unhappy?" Alex ventured. "Maybe he's blackmailing Hildy into giving him a place to stay?"

"No, she's smiling," Paige replied, sorry to disappoint him. "If we turn Stanley in, could she be charged as an accessory or something?"

"I don't know," Alex replied. "But we're not turning him over to anyone until I get a chance to search for that tape."

She leaned forward, lowering her voice. "How are you going to manage that?"

"I don't know yet," Alex said. "But now that we're this close I have to give it a try."

"What if you get caught?"

"I hardly think Wally Stanislawski will want to call the police on me."

Paige didn't know what to think, but it was obvious Alex was determined to go through with it.

"What's he doing now?" Alex asked her.

"He just finished his eggs, but he's sifting through the bacon. Mom always said her second husband was the finickiest eater."

"He's not the only one," Alex observed. "You've hardly touched a bite of your breakfast."

Paige didn't want to tell him that the anticipation he had mentioned the night before had stolen her appetite. The hunger inside of her had nothing to do with food and everything to do with the man seated across the table from her.

Then her attention was drawn back to Stanley. "Oh, he's getting up now. It looks like he's leaving."

Alex tossed his napkin on the table and rose to his feet. "Wait here."

"Where are you..." But he was already out of earshot, following in Stanley's footsteps.

Paige waited for what seemed like an interminable amount of time before Alex finally came back and sat down at the table.

"Stanley's staying here in room number three," Alex said, "directly across the hall from our room. I followed him there and saw him use a key to get inside his room. Then I checked outside and there's a trellis leading up the side of the house directly to his window."

"Are you crazy?" she said, slapping the newspaper down in front of her. "You'll break your neck if you try to climb up a trellis."

"Do you have a better idea?"

"As a matter of fact, I do." She pushed her plate away. "I'll search Stanley's room as soon as the coast is clear. You can follow him and run interference in case he tries to come back to his room too soon. He's never seen you before, so he won't be suspicious if you start up some small talk."

"Hold it," Alex said, "you are *not* breaking into his room. In the first place, you don't know how to get in."

"Yes, I do." She dug into her purse and held up a credit card. "My mother and I lived in an old apartment building with the same kind of doors before we moved in with my grandfather. I was always forgetting my key, so I learned how to use a credit card to get in. It worked like a charm every time."

He didn't seem to share her enthusiasm. "In the second place, I don't want you putting yourself in danger. I'm the one who wanted to go after Stanley. I'm also the one who's physically more capable of handling him if he goes on the attack."

"Stanley's not a fighter," Paige assured him. "I'll be fine. Especially if you're running interference."

Alex met her gaze and she could see the concern there. And the love. "It's too damn risky."

So was falling in love with him. But Paige was determined to get her man. First Stanley.

Then Alex.

13

"I WANT YOU TO get in and get out as soon as possible," Alex told her, still not happy with their arrangement. They'd gone over the plan at least ten time in the last hour while waiting for Stanley to emerge from his room. "Fifteen minutes at the most. Ten would be even better."

"Give me twenty minutes," she said calmly. "If necessary, do something to distract Stanley so I have enough time."

"And if I can't stop him?"

"Shh," she ordered, turning to open the door a crack. "I think I hear something."

The distinct squeal of dry door hinges sounded directly across the hall from them. Then Stanley emerged from his room, dressed in a dapper gray suit and a green silk tie that matched his eyes. His hair was slicked back and the aroma of expensive cologne filtered into their room.

"Looks like somebody has a date," Paige whispered as they watched Stanley head for the staircase. Then she turned around and flashed a smile at Alex. "Wish me luck."

He grabbed her and kissed her, propelling her back against the wall. Raw heat sizzled between them, threatening to explode as he rocked his body into hers. She moaned at the sensation and he was seriously tempted to seduce her right out of this crazy idea.

He pulled back instead, ready to finish this business with Stanley Weaver so he and Paige could concentrate on each other. "Twenty minutes," he ordered, "and not a second more."

Then Alex took off down the hallway without looking back, leaving Paige behind to do the dirty work. He stayed about fifty paces behind Weaver as he followed the man out of the bed-and-breakfast and down the street—far enough not to raise suspicion, but close enough to keep him in sight.

Five blocks later, Stanley walked into a small jewelry store nestled between a bakery and a coffee shop. Alex looked around, then ducked into a bookstore across the street. He grabbed a bestseller off the shelf, then leafed through it, standing near the plate glass window so he could keep an eye on Stanley.

He could see Weaver bent over a large glass display case, an attentive clerk assisting him on the other side. Perhaps Stanley had found another potential wife to add to his collection and was looking for the perfect engagement ring to sweep her off her feet. Or he could be simply spending some of the blackmail money that he'd collected over the years.

Ten minutes. The time slowly ticked by, with Alex growing more worried with each passing second. What if Hildy walked in on Paige? Or Weaver had the tapes booby trapped?

"May I help you?" a young clerk asked. She wasn't more than nineteen, with a shock of orange-red hair and a ring in her nose.

"No thanks, I'm just browsing," Alex said, glancing back at the jewelry store. Weaver was still inside, though he and the clerk had moved to another counter.

"So do you like women on top?" the girl asked.

Alex blinked, then looked at her. "What?"

She nodded toward the book in his hand. *"Women On Top—An Insider's Guide to Female CEOs."*

He glanced down at the cover. "Oh, sure. My favorite subject."

"Really?" The clerk beamed at him. "Then you should try Kit Hollister. She has some great books on gender inequity in the workplace. Or Silva Isaacson, if you want the history of the glass ceiling."

"Maybe some other time," Alex said absently, glancing back at the jewelry store window across the street. The clouds had parted and the sun now reflected off the glass, making it hard to see inside, though he'd kept his eye on the door the whole time.

"Just let me know when," the clerk said with a flirtatious smile. "I'm here every Monday, Wednesday, Thursday and Saturday."

"Thanks." He set the book back on the shelf, then walked outside, apprehension prickling his spine. He moved across the street, then peered through the jewelry store window, his hands cupped around his eyes.

The clerk was the only person he saw inside. Stepping away from the window, Alex looked up and down the street, though he was positive the man hadn't come out the door.

So where was he?

Walking into the jewelry store, he approached the clerk. "I'm looking for a man who was just in here. Dark hair and bifocals, about this tall." He raised his hand to shoulder level.

"Oh, he went out the back," the clerk said, hitching a thumb over his shoulder. "Said he thought somebody was following him." Then the clerk's eyes widened. "Are you following him?"

But Alex didn't stick around to answer the question. He raced out the door and ran toward Hildy's place, hoping like hell he wasn't too late.

PAIGE STEPPED into Stanley's room and closed the door behind her, slipping her credit card into the back pocket of her blue jeans.

Then she paused to take a deep breath, trying to gather her equilibrium after that scorching kiss. How had she ever thought she could resist Alex? All he had to do was touch her and she was on fire.

As soon as this mess with Stanley was settled, she

was going to return the favor. She looked at her watch, noting that she only had eighteen minutes left.

The layout of the room was identical to the one she shared with Alex. Same double bed. Same closet. Same window seat. It even had a fireplace and a private bath.

A thorough, methodical search would take the full twenty minutes so Paige knew she didn't have a second to waste. Starting at the closet, she carefully searched through Stanley's suitcases and leather valise, noting that he was as much of a pack rat as ever. It gave her hope that she'd find the tapes before her twenty minutes were up.

But they weren't in the closet. She hastily repacked everything, not having the time to leave the room exactly as she'd found it. Stanley would never notice the additional clutter. And if he did, so be it. He deserved a little paranoia after what he'd put Alex and her mother through, not to mention the customers he'd blackmailed. It still made her furious to think about it.

So she was less than gentle when she sorted through the collection of custom-made suits hanging in his closet. No doubt paid for by his victims. His designer ties lay tangled on the floor like a nest of snakes by the time she was through.

Paige moved to the bed next, all too aware of the minutes ticking by. She looked between the mattress and the box spring, as well as under the bed itself. But all she found there was a herd of dust bunnies. She checked the feather pillows for any suspicious bulges, then moved onto the nightstand, sifting through every drawer.

But no tapes.

Growing discouraged, Paige checked her watch. She had five minutes left. Just time enough to search the window seat. Grabbing the yellow gingham pillows one by one, she crushed them between her hands, hoping to feel some hard edges inside. But each one passed the squeeze test. Then she opened the lid of the window seat, finding a spare blanket inside, just as she had in her own room.

Pulling the blanket out, she shook it open, but no tapes fell to the floor. She'd so wanted to deliver that blackmail tape to Alex. To finally be able to put the past behind them and move on with their lives. Instead they'd reached another dead end.

Releasing a sigh of disappointment, she folded the blanket again. It was much smaller than the one in her room; thinner too. Yet it barely fit into a window seat of the exact same dimensions as the one in her room.

Paige tossed the blanket aside, then knelt down to get a closer look at the storage compartment. It looked solid, but it was much shallower than the other one. When she pressed her hand against the bottom, the wood shifted just a little.

A false bottom?

Her pulse picked up as she manipulated the

wood, looking for a lever or a pull to pop it off. Her time limit was up but she couldn't stop now; not when she was so close.

At last her fingertips brushed across a slight imperfection in the grain of the wood. She pressed hard there and one side of the wooden panel magically lifted into the air. Prying it open, Paige looked inside.

She'd found it.

Inside the bottom of the window seat was a cigar box full of miniature cassette tapes, each one marked with the name of a plant. That confused her for a moment, until she saw one identified by the name of a rare, exotic plant that had graced Lucian Mackopoulos's private office.

Stuffing the cigar box in the tote bag she'd brought with her, Paige hastily returned the window seat to normal, even arranging the gingham pillows on top.

Adrenaline pumped through her veins from the thrill of the hunt—and her success. She couldn't wait to show the tapes to Alex. To see the expression on his face when she told him she wanted the two of them to have a second chance.

For real this time.

But that thought was lost when she heard a key in the lock.

Paige frantically looked around for somewhere to hide, finally deciding that she was most likely to avoid detection under the bed. She dove under the box spring, tugging her tote bag out of sight just as Stanley walked into the room. She lay flat on her stomach, her head turned toward the door.

What had happened to Alex?

Panic welled inside of her as Stanley walked toward the bed. His black leather shoes were only inches from her face. Then she heard the jingle of keys hitting the quilt top. She released her deep, pent-up breath when he walked away again, silently gasping for fresh air.

Stanley began to whistle as he moved about the room, a man without a care in the world. She followed the path of those black shoes, her heart skipping a beat when he paused in front of the window seat. Had she left something askew? A telltale sign that alerted him to the fact that she'd found his illegal treasure trove.

If so, a knock at the door diverted his attention. She held her breath, hoping it was Alex on the other side coming to her rescue. Instead, Hildy walked into the room.

"What's this I hear about you seeing Lorna Swenson?"

"Well, good afternoon to you, too, big sister."

Paige could see Hildy's sensible orthopedic shoes come toe-to-toe with his designer ones.

"Please stay away from Lorna, Wally. She's one of my dearest friends and a member of my church circle. I don't want you to hurt her."

"Who said anything about hurting her?" he said cheerfully. "I think she's a lovely woman."

But Hildy wasn't buying it. "Lorna just lost her husband six months ago. She's vulnerable."

"She's lonely," Stanley countered. "Don't you want her to be happy?"

Hildy walked over to the window, not saying anything for a long moment. "You were only two years old when our mother died, Wally, and I promised her that I would take good care of you."

"And you always have," he said, walking up behind her. "Giving me a place to stay during the tough times. I simply couldn't make it without you, Hildy."

She turned around to face him. "I just don't understand why you have to get involved with all these women. You're a charmer, Wally, you always have been. Even I'm not immune to it."

"You've always been so good to me," Wally said, exercising some of that charm now. "I want to change, I really do. But I need help."

"You know I'll always help you if I can."

"I need some money," he said.

She sighed. "Again?"

"Not a lot," he assured her. "Just enough for me to go back to podiatry school. I really think that's my calling, Hildy. And I can pay you back as soon as I graduate."

Paige could see those sensible shoes pacing back

and forth across the floor. "How much do you need this time?"

"I think five thousand should cover all my initial expenses."

She couldn't believe it. Hildy was as much Stanley's victim as all the other women in his life. Paige hadn't thought it possible to dislike the man any more than she already did, but the way he was manipulating his sister made her sick.

"And you'll break it off with Lorna?" she asked hopefully.

"As soon as you write the check," he promised. "I won't have time for romance if I'm going to school full-time. And this time, I'm going to graduate."

"You've said that before...."

"This time will be different," he assured her. "I promise on our mother's grave."

"Dr. Wally Stanislawski does have a nice ring to it," Hildy said, buying into the fantasy. At a cost of five thousand dollars.

"I'll go tell Lorna it's over." He reached out to hug his sister. "Then I'm going to take off for a few days. I've got this funny feeling that's someone's watching me."

"Oh, Wally."

"Don't worry," he said, "I'll be all right. And I'm going to make you proud, Hildy, just you wait and see."

"I hope so, Wally," Hildy said under her breath

as her brother walked out of his room. "I really hope so."

Hildy soon followed him, closing the door behind her. Paige strained her ears, listening to the fading echo of footsteps. Then she pulled herself out from under the bed and stood up, wiping the dust off her shirt and slacks. Grabbing her tote bag, she cracked open the door to see if the coast was clear.

But Alex was the only one there. He pushed open the door, then swept her into his arms, squeezing her so tightly that Paige couldn't breathe.

"Thank God you're here," he whispered against her ear.

"I got the tapes and—"

But Alex wouldn't let her finish. He lifted her feet off the floor and carried her back to their room, kicking the door shut behind him.

"Are you all right?" he asked, setting her on the floor. His hands moved frantically over her body as if he was checking for injuries.

"I'm fine," she said, then held up the tote bag. "And I found the tapes!"

Alex took the tote bag out of her hand and tossed it onto the floor. "At this moment, I don't give a damn about any blackmail tapes. You have no idea what's been going through my mind when I realized Stanley was in that room with you. Did he find you? Hurt you?" A muscle flexed in his jaw. "If he laid one hand on you, I'll..."

Paige placed her fingers over his mouth, a frisson of electricity shooting through her body at the contact. "I'm fine, Alex. Really. And the only man I want laying his hands on me is you. Now."

14

ALEX DIDN'T THINK it was not possible to shift from terrified panic to sheer lust in under ten seconds, but Paige managed to bring him to that state with a few simple words.

"You want my hands on you?" he echoed, wanting to make sure he'd heard her right. Blood rushed south, pooling hot and heavy in his groin.

"Oh, yeah," she said huskily, stepping close to him. "All over me. Like this."

She reached out to brush her hands over his chest, her fingers slipping between the buttons of his shirt to tease and tantalize the skin underneath. The buttons popped off, one by one, as she widened her exploration.

Soon his shirt hung open and she leaned forward to press her lips against one flat nipple, circling it with her tongue while her hands slid down his belly over his hips, leaving no doubt as to her destination.

He sucked in a sharp breath when she wrapped her fingers around his erection. His head fell back as Paige molded the hard length of him around the cotton fabric of his slacks, stroking and exploring until his breath came in uneven gasps.

Then he heard the sound of his own zipper and knew he was about to explode before she even got his pants off. It had been so long and he wanted her so much.

"Slow down," he implored, fighting for control. He took her hands in his own before it was too late. Then he led her to the bed.

She looked up at him with big blue eyes. Now it was his turn to stimulate and seduce and Alex intended to take his sweet time.

"Where do you want me to touch you first?" he asked, kneeling on the bed beside her.

"Here." She brought his hands to her breasts, her eyelids sweeping shut as his palms closed around her.

That was all the direction he needed. He kissed her long and deep while his fingers ignited slow burning fires all over her body. She moaned into his mouth as he shed her blouse, then her bra. The rest of her clothes followed in short order, along with his.

When they were both naked, Alex pulled back to look at her stretched out before him on the bed.

"Beautiful," he murmured, leaning down to kiss the top of one breast. Then he moved lower to kiss her knee. "So beautiful."

His lips grazed her inner thigh as he began a sensual exploration of her body with his mouth that made her cry out for him. Paige reached up to wrap her hands around the iron rails on the headboard, opening herself up to him.

"Now, Alex," she gasped, as he moved over the top of her.

He pounded with need, barely able to roll on a condom before he sank into her with a groan of sheer ecstasy. Then he rolled over so she lay on top of him. He wanted to watch her as she rocked against him, relishing the sweet friction of their bodies moving in rhythm together.

She gazed down at him, her eyes glazed with love and lust and something more. Something that made him truly believe in forever.

Paige tried to hold back, to let this exquisite moment linger between them. But the waves of pleasure kept licking at her flesh as Alex moved deep inside of her. His broad hands molded to her breasts, his thumbs sensuously circling her nipples.

The waves swelled and crested until Paige cried out as a tidal wave engulfed her. She quivered at the awesome intensity of her climax, collapsing onto his broad chest.

Alex held her tightly against him, rocking against her once more before thrusting into her with a hoarse cry of release. But he still didn't let her go.

She lay on top of him until they were both breathing normally once again. Then she propped her elbow up on his chest and looked down into his handsome face.

"That was nice."

He arched a brow. "Nice?"

She laughed, joy welling up inside of her. "Maybe nice is an understatement."

He slid his hands down her bare back until he cupped her buttocks. "There's no maybe about it. We're incredible together."

Paige was glad she wasn't the only one who thought so. Her experience with men was rather limited, but something told her what she and Alex had just shared only came along once or twice in a lifetime.

"So incredible," he continued, "that I think we should start planning our future together."

Paige wanted that more than anything, but they needed to put the past behind them once and for all. "I want to spend the rest of my life with you, Alex Mackopoulos, but first we have to decide what to do about Stanley."

Alex rolled onto his back and stared up at the ceiling. "I can't turn those tapes of my father over to the police, Paige. We'll have to find some other way to bring him down."

She propped her head against the pillow, laying one hand on his chest. For some reason, she couldn't stop touching him.

"I know. Frankly, I don't think we should turn any of the tapes I found over to the police. They're full of personal secrets that Stanley's victims paid big money to hide. Secrets that could destroy lives."

"If I had my way, we'd burn every last one of them."

"Then why don't we?" She looked over at the fireplace, a small blaze crackling in the hearth.

Alex stared at her. "Destroy the evidence?"

"Maybe that's illegal," she said, trying to determine the right and wrong in this situation. "I don't know. All I do know is that Stanley used my business to invade the privacy of unsuspecting customers like your father."

"There's something else to consider," he said. "If those tapes are turned over to the police, the reputation of your flower shop will suffer."

"It would probably put me out of business," she replied, then bit her lower lip. "Does that make me selfish?"

"No, it makes you human," Alex replied, reaching out to brush his knuckles across her cheek. "Besides, according to Ed Rooney, Stanley is already wanted on several outstanding warrants, so he's going to jail whether we turn these tapes over or not."

"All we have to do is turn him in."

"I can't think of anything that would give me greater pleasure." Then his hand drifted from her face and moved lower. "Well, maybe one thing."

"Soon," she promised, leaning over to kiss him. "I want to call Rooney and have him get in touch with his contact at the police department. Stanley's leaving in the morning so they'll have to make the arrest tonight."

"He is?"

She nodded. "He conned his own sister into giving him five thousand dollars in return for not bilking one of her good friends. The amazing thing is how Hildy still wants to believe her brother can reform by going to podiatry school. It's sad, really."

"It's hard to accept the flaws in your own family," Alex said softly and she knew he was talking about more than the dysfunctional Stanislawskis.

Paige sat up and reached for the tote bag, handing it to him. "All the tapes are in there. I brought a recorder along if you want to listen to it to make sure."

He gave a brisk nod, but didn't open the bag.

Paige got out of bed, aware of Alex's gaze lingering on her naked body. "I'll give you some privacy."

"Don't be gone too long."

Paige grabbed her cell phone off the nightstand and padded into the bathroom. She didn't know the Mackopoulos family secret, but she could see the shame in his eyes when he spoke of the tapes. He'd been ashamed enough to go to jail for a year rather than expose his father in a court of law.

Alex Mackopoulos was a proud man. Not to mention stubborn, loyal and sexy as hell.

And she'd never let him go again.

FIFTEEN MINUTES LATER, Alex stood in front of the hearth, watching the flames consume the minicassette tapes Paige had found in Stanley's room. He'd listened to as much of his father's tapes as he could stomach before throwing them into the fire, along with the rest of the tapes in the bag.

He still couldn't comprehend how Lucian Mackopoulos could cheat on Thea. Especially with women named Lola and Carmen and Rita. It puzzled him since he was just beginning to understand the special bond that formed between a man and a woman who shared a bed. A life. A family. He'd truly believed his parents had shared that same kind of bond. But those tapes proved otherwise.

One thing was for certain. Alex would never follow in his father's footsteps. Paige was the only woman for him. He couldn't wait to watch her belly swell with his child. To raise a family with her. To do so many of the things with her that he'd dreamed about while he was in jail.

She came up behind him and wrapped her arms around his waist. "Are you all right?"

He turned around to hold her. "I'm better now that you're here. Although I'm not sure I approve of that robe you have on. I prefer you naked."

She smiled. "This from a man who is wearing polka-dot boxer shorts."

He pulled her closer to him. "Hey, I have a long night ahead planned for us. I didn't want any flying sparks to put a damper on the evening."

She laughed. "That's what I love about you, Alex. You're always ready for action."

He didn't move. "You love me?"

She met his gaze and he saw her love reflected in her blue eyes. "Now and always."

He kissed her as the fire popped and crackled behind them. The taste of her inflamed him and his hands fumbled with the belt of her robe, loosening the tie.

"The police are on their way to pick up Stanley," she warned. "Ed said they should be here sometime within the next hour or so."

"They won't bother us," he promised her, parting the lapels of her robe to reveal her creamy shoulders. He leaned down to kiss the tiny freckles there.

Her eyes fluttered shut. "You don't think...they'll want to take the statements of the guests?"

"I hope not," he said, his mouth moving lower as the robe slipped off her shoulders and pooled onto the floor. "Because I don't feel like talking right now."

She tilted her head back as his mouth found her breast. "Me, neither."

They made slow, sweet love on the thick rug in front of the fireplace, losing all sense of time as they concentrated only on each other. Sometime later, the sound of a commotion outside brought them both to the window.

Alex slipped a robe over Paige's shoulders, then grabbed his own as she parted the curtain to look down on the street below. Two police cruisers, lights flashing, sat parked at an angle with Stanley's car trapped in between them.

"They must have been waiting for him to return from his date with the widow Swenson," Paige said, wrapping her arms around her waist. "Poor Hildy."

Alex spotted Stanley's sister standing outside in a pink wrapper, wringing her hands together as she talked with a cop. Her brother stood sullenly behind one of the cruisers, his hands cuffed behind his back. He looked up at the house, his gaze narrowing as he fixed on their window.

Paige started back, the curtain falling from her hand. "I think he saw me."

Alex set his hands on her shoulders. "It's all right. He can't hurt either one of us anymore."

"I know," she said, putting Stanley out of her mind forever. Paige turned into his arms, her body fitting perfectly against his own. He didn't think it was possible to desire her again this soon, but his arousal proved otherwise.

"I love you," she whispered, laying her cheek against his chest.

He kissed the top of her head, his throat growing tight. Not many people got a second chance and most didn't deserve one. Alex didn't know if he deserved a woman like Paige, but he wanted her all the same. And he'd make damn sure she didn't regret it.

"I love you, too," he said huskily. "Now let's go back to bed."

THE NEXT DAY, Paige and Alex spent the entire trip back to San Francisco planning their future together. She was almost giddy with excitement, letting herself believe, for the first time, that she and Alex might actually have their own happily ever after.

"I want you to keep taking those college classes," Alex insisted as they pulled into her driveway. "I'll help out at the flower shop whenever you need me."

"But won't you be too busy with the new line of spas your friend Tony is opening up?"

"Not too busy for my wife." He shut off the engine and leaned over to kiss her. "I can't wait to marry you."

She arched a brow. "Then why can't we get married before September?"

"Because I cheated you out of the last wedding," Alex said, popping open his door. "I want to do this one right. A big Greek wedding with all the frills."

Paige followed him to the trunk of the car. "Five months seems so far away."

He retrieved her suitcase from the trunk, then turned to face her. "Nothing is going to stop our marriage this time, Paige. I promise you."

"I know," she replied, tempted to tell him she didn't need a big crowd to witness their vows. After the chaos of the wedding that wasn't, Paige preferred the idea of a small, intimate ceremony with just their families present.

But when she'd gingerly broached the subject with Alex, he'd been adamant about giving her a big, splashy wedding, even larger than the one they'd planned before. She knew he still felt guilty over the chaos he'd caused in her life with that botched ceremony.

What he didn't understand is that she didn't need a fancy wedding to make her happy. She just needed him.

"Looks like your mom has company," Alex said as he walked her to the house.

Paige had noticed the silver Ford parked on the street, too, right in front of Ed Rooney's Oldsmobile. "That's strange. Mom should be at the shop. Unless Ed is meeting someone here on his own."

"Maybe the producer for his show or even a cameraman," Alex ventured. "Now that Stanley Weaver's been arrested, the mystery of his disappearance has finally been solved."

"And not a UFO in sight," she said as, laughing, they both walked into the house. Then she saw Ed pacing back and forth across the living floor and her laughter faded.

Ed stopped walking when he saw them, worry etched on his craggy face. "I've been trying to call you on your cell phone for hours."

"The battery is dead," she explained, not revealing that they'd been too busy making love last night to plug it in. "Is something wrong?"

"I'm not sure where to start," Ed said, running a

hand through his sparse hair. "Your mother's been arrested."

Her mouth fell open. "What?"

Alex set down her suitcase. "How did that happen?"

"I think both of you had better sit down for this one," Rooney said, glancing over his shoulder. "We don't have much time."

"I don't understand," Paige said, taking a seat on the sofa. Alex sat beside her, his presence a calming contrast to the panic in Ed's eyes.

"It happened just a few hours ago," he explained. "The police showed up at Bay Bouquets with a search warrant. They turned the place upside down until they found what they were looking for."

She was almost afraid to ask. "What did they find?"

He took a deep breath. "Audiotapes. Apparently, Stanislawski wants to cut a deal with the state. He's claiming you and your mother arranged a blackmail scheme to cheat your customers out of thousands of dollars."

"But we burned those tapes," Paige said, as a strange man walked out of the kitchen, pocketing his cell phone.

He flashed at badge at her. "Looks like you didn't burn all of them, Ms. Hanover. We found the tapes you stashed in the drop ceiling at your business. Now you're under arrest for extortion."

She looked frantically at Alex as the cop hauled her to her feet. "This is insane!"

Alex stood up beside her, his face flushed with anger. "You've got it all wrong. Stanley Weaver is setting up Paige and her mother. The man is scum. Can't you see that?"

But the policeman ignored them both. "You have the right to remain silent. Anything you say may be held against you in a court of law. You have the right to an attorney. If you cannot afford an attorney, one will be provided for you...."

Paige stood there in shock as the cop cuffed her, then led her out the door as he recited the rest of the Miranda warning. Her mind spun and all she could think about was her mother sitting in a jail cell somewhere. Would Paige even get to see her? To talk to her?

Alex followed them out the door. "I'll call a lawyer, Paige. We'll get you cleared of these ridiculous charges before the day is out. I promise."

She didn't say anything as the cop guided her into the back seat of his car. Alex stood helplessly on the front lawn as the car pulled away and she had the worst foreboding that she'd never see him again.

Paige knew Alex couldn't get involved with this mess. Not without the truth about his father's secret coming out. He'd gone to jail himself to keep that from happening.

She took a deep breath, then another, mentally urging herself to calm down. Everything would be all right. It had to be. Stanley was simply making up some story to make himself look good. He must have planted those tapes in her ceiling a long time ago as some sort of insurance policy, with Paige and her mother as his dupes. Or maybe it was simply revenge for her turning him in to the police.

What if he succeeded?

Then she'd lose everything. Her flower business. Her home. Alex. There'd be no September wedding. She and Margo would both be serving time in jail for a crime they didn't commit. Stanley's crime.

She wanted to believe that Alex would help her find a way out of this trap, but the same feelings of shock and betrayal that she'd experienced when he'd left her at the altar a year ago flowed through her now.

Family always comes first for a Mackopoulos. Nico's words echoed in her mind. Alex had told her the same thing. What if Nico was right? What if Alex decided it was better to wash his hands of her than drag his family into this mess?

She slammed her eyes shut, pushing those traitorous thoughts out of her head. Alex loved her. She had to keep believing in him. He wouldn't let her down.

Would he?

15

ALEX STOOD on Paige's front lawn, still staring down the street long after the unmarked police car had disappeared with the woman he loved handcuffed inside. He felt as if he'd been sucker punched, his gut churning with dread for her.

Ed Rooney walked up beside him. "We've got to do something."

Alex drew a deep breath, ready to take action. "I'm open to suggestions."

"First, tell me what the hell Paige meant about burning some tapes," Ed said. "That's the last thing we needed that cop to hear."

"Paige searched Stanislawski's room before we called you last night," Alex explained, "and found all the master tapes. We both agreed it would be better to burn them than to find all those deep, personal secrets splashed across the front page of the *San Francisco Chronicle*."

"It's a little too late for that," Ed bit out. "This story is hot. One of my contacts at the station told me the tapes they found involve some of the most powerful people in this city. A few of them have already agreed to testify in the case."

Hope sprang in his chest. "Then they can prove that neither Paige nor her mother were involved. It was all Stanley."

Ed shook his head. "Just the opposite, I'm afraid. No one ever actually saw Stanley. He used a device to alter his voice when he called with his demands, then had the money delivered to a post-office box he'd opened in Margo's name."

"Damn."

"You can say that again." Ed sighed. "Because Margo was married to that scum, everyone believes she must have been involved. Paige as well, since she owned the business. You know how people love conspiracy theories. According to one of my contacts, Stanislawski is claiming he was simply the legman in the whole operation."

"But he's the one with the criminal record."

"The problem is that this crime doesn't fit his profile," Ed replied. "Before marrying Margo, he stuck to bilking lonely widows out of their savings accounts. Purely petty stuff. Extortion is big time and, unfortunately, the tapes and the combination to the post-office box were found in the flower shop. That's all the cops needed to make an arrest."

"But is it enough to go to trial?" Alex asked, hoping to find a way out.

"I don't know," Ed said, squinting up at Alex. "Are you willing to take that chance?"

Ed knew Alex had information about the black-mail scheme. Paige had mentioned it to him over the phone yesterday to explain why they'd gone after Stanley on their own. Ed obviously thought Alex could testify in Paige and Margo's behalf and reveal everything he knew.

Including all his father's dirty secrets.

"I have to go," Alex said, heading toward his car. "Find a good lawyer for Paige and Margo."

"Already done," Ed called after him. "The preliminary hearing is set for ten o'clock tomorrow morning."

"I'll be there," Alex promised, then climbed into his car and peeled out of the driveway.

It was one promise he wouldn't break.

By the time he arrived home, Alex knew what he had to do. Paige needed him. He couldn't let her down. But that didn't make the task before him any easier.

He walked into the foyer and started up the stairs.

"Hold it," Nico said, standing in the doorway of the drawing room. "Where do you think you're going?"

Alex stopped to catch his breath. "I need to talk to Mom."

"She had one of her migraines this morning," Nico informed him. "She's upstairs resting right now, so it will have to wait."

"It can't wait," Alex countered. "It's time to tell Mom the truth, Nico. Paige and her mother have been arrested for a crime they didn't commit. Duplicates of the blackmail tapes have been found. The truth is going to come out anyway."

"No, it's not," Nico said, pulling some microcassettes from his shirt pocket. "The police were here earlier. They told me about the bust at Bay Bouquets."

"And they gave you the duplicates?" Alex asked incredulously.

Nico nodded. "They don't need them since Dad isn't available as a witness. The cop I talked to said there are other victims who are willing to come forward. Not all of them, but enough."

Alex climbed down the stairs to face his brother. "Didn't you hear me? Paige and Margo weren't involved. They shouldn't have to pay for Weaver's crimes."

Nico scowled at him. "They won't. Anyone with a brain can see this is a setup. They'll get off."

"Maybe," Alex replied. "But there aren't any guarantees. If there's enough evidence to arrest them, a jury might believe there's enough evidence to convict them."

Nico's jaw tightened. "If that happens, we can come forward after the trial. I don't want our mother humiliated in a public courtroom."

"Neither do I," Alex bit out. "You know I'd never do anything to intentionally hurt her. But I can't just turn my back on Paige. I won't. She's the woman I love. The woman I plan to marry."

"So now she comes first in your life?" Nico shook his head. "I don't understand how you could turn your back on your own family."

"Because I love her," he said simply. "Maybe that's something you can't understand. Our father sure as hell didn't understand love or he never would have betrayed his wife the way he did. If you want to blame someone, blame him."

Nico didn't say anything, but Alex could see he'd hit a nerve.

"I don't like this any better than you do," Alex said, calmer now. He understood his brother's position even if he didn't agree with it. "But my decision is made. I'm here to tell our mother the truth. I want her to hear it from me."

"Hear what?" Thea asked, standing at the top of the stairs. She reached for the handrail and slowly descended, her eyes still slightly puffy from her nap.

Nico turned to him. "We'll both tell her."

Alex nodded as they escorted their mother into the drawing room. When she was seated in a chair, he walked over to the window, looking out at the garden she loved so much. This was even harder than he thought.

"Tell me, Alex," Thea said at last. "I always know when something is troubling you."

He glanced at Nico, then at Thea again. "This isn't easy to say."

Worry clouded her eyes. "What's wrong? Are

you sick?" She turned to his brother. "Or is it Nico? You look a little pale."

"We're both fine," Nico assured her. "This is about Dad."

She sat back in her chair, her curiosity piqued. "What about him?"

Alex knew there were no perfect words to break the news to her, so he quit searching for them and just stated it bluntly. "Dad had an affair."

"With your mother, twenty-nine years ago," Thea said, looking more puzzled than ever. "I know, dear. That's ancient history."

Nico shook his head. "No, Mom, there were other affairs. Much more recent than twenty-nine years ago. They were recorded on tape at his office."

She blanched. "Recorded on tape?"

"Audiotape," Alex clarified. "A man named Stanley Weaver hid a recording device in a potted plant in Dad's office, then resorted to blackmail when he got evidence of the affairs on tape. I only listened to a few seconds of each one. That's all it took to figure out what was going on."

Thea covered her face with her hands. "I don't believe this."

"I know it's a shock," Alex said, aching for her. "But..."

"What were their names?" Thea interjected, lowering her hands to reveal her distraught face.

"I only heard first names," he said, hoping he could get through this before she broke down.

"Their names don't even really matter. What matters is that Nico and I paid the blackmailer twenty thousand dollars so no one would ever know."

"We just wanted to protect you," Nico said. "To keep you from ever finding out."

"Twenty thousand dollars," she said in disbelief. "To protect me." Then she looked up at Alex. "That's how much money went missing from the company."

"I used it to pay off the extortion," Nico confessed. "I meant to pay it back right away but everything started spinning out of control with Dad's illness and the company and the investigation. Alex got called before the grand jury, but we both agreed that he couldn't tell them where the money went."

"To protect me?" She stared at Alex. "That's why you went to jail. Just to protect me from hearing those tapes?"

He'd never wanted her to know the truth. But now he couldn't keep it from her any longer. "Yes."

Thea slumped back in her chair. "I don't believe this is happening. I want you to tell me the names of these women you think your father had an affair with."

She was in denial. Hardly surprising, considering everything they'd just told her.

"The names don't matter, Mom."

"Tell me!"

He took a deep breath. "There was a Lola. A Carmen. And a Rita."

"I knew it," she breathed, then muttered something in Greek that Alex couldn't quite make out. But he heard a few choice words that weren't used in polite Greek company.

"You know those women?" Nico ventured.

"Yes, I know them." She rose to her feet. "I *am* them!"

Alex and Nico exchanged glances, each wondering if the shock of her husband's betrayal had sent her over the edge.

"My son in jail!" Thea exclaimed, sounding almost hysterical. "Twenty thousand dollars! All because your father and I had an adventurous sex life!"

"So you didn't mind the affairs," Alex said slowly, still trying to understand.

"Those weren't affairs!" A deep blush suffused her cheeks. "I'd go to Lucian's office sometimes and pretend to be a stranger named Lola or Carmen or Rita. It's called sexual role-playing." She held up both hands. "Something I do *not* want to discuss with my sons in the room."

Alex stared at his stepmother, almost as embarrassed as she was. "You mean it was you and Dad on those tapes...."

"Yes," she admitted, thoroughly exasperated now. "And if you two would have just come to me in the first place, none of this would have happened! When will you men get it through your thick Greek skulls that I'm not some fainting flower that needs protection. Look at the problems it has caused this family."

Nico started toward her. "Mom, calm down."

She held him off. "Don't you tell me what to do, young man." Then she planted her hands on her hips and looked between the two of them. "Exactly how long ago did this blackmail scheme take place?"

Alex and Nico exchanged guilty glances. "Well over a year ago."

"So why have you suddenly decided to bring it to my attention now? What's going on?"

Alex launched into a lengthy explanation about his relationship with Paige, starting from the beginning when he'd "accidentally" bumped into her on the wharf over a year ago to her arrest today. Nico confessed his part too, including the e-mail proposal he'd sent to her in Alex's name. All in an effort to discover the whereabouts of Stanley Weaver and his blackmail tapes.

"And this girl still wants to marry you after everything you've put her through?" Thea asked in amazement.

"Yes," Alex replied, hoping it was still true. He hadn't been able to see or talk to Paige since her arrest. "As incredible as it is to believe, Paige is willing to give me a second chance."

"Then she must love you as much as I loved your father," Thea said, reaching out to cup her son's cheek. "But I'll have to warn her about Greek men."

"I just hope you get the chance." Alex pulled Thea into a hug. "I have to go to the police and tell them about the blackmail tapes, Mom. I'm not even sure how much it will help Paige, since neither Nico nor I had any direct dealings with Weaver." He closed his eyes, unwilling to contemplate that possibility. "If there was any other way..."

"There is," Thea told him. "I did meet Mr. Weaver face-to-face. And I have proof that will exonerate your fiancée that I'll be happy to give to you." She tilted up her chin. "For a price."

"What price?" he asked warily.

"You and Paige come to dinner every Sunday at my house for one year after you're married. I want to get to know my new daughter-in-law and teach her how to cook good Greek food."

"You can teach both of us," Alex said, leaning down to kiss her cheek. "And Nico, too. He'll need all the help he can get finding a woman."

"My Nico will find the right girl," Thea assured him, reaching up to pat her oldest son's shoulder. "All in good time."

Alex couldn't stand the suspense any longer. "So what proof do you have that will clear Paige?"

Thea walked over to the rolltop desk and unlocked the top drawer. Then she pulled out a videotape.

"That's the tape of Dad's memorial service," Nico observed.

"Yes," Thea confirmed, "and if you watch it,

you'll see a man approach me shortly after the service is over and offer me revealing audiotapes of my late husband that he promised would help me overcome my grief. All for a price, of course."

"That scum," Nico breathed.

Thea nodded. "Naturally, I wasn't interested, but now I'm willing to bet that man was Stanley Weaver. If it was, I'll be more than happy to testify against him in court."

"Why didn't you tell us about this?" Alex asked.

She sighed. "I suppose because I was trying to protect you."

"I think this family's been keeping too many secrets," Nico said wryly.

Thea held up the tape. "Then let's go put an end to all this nonsense once and for all."

16

PAIGE SAT at the defense table with her mother waiting for the preliminary hearing to begin while their lawyer stood at the bench with the judge and the assistant district attorney.

Rina Halpern was a no-nonsense trial lawyer originally from Boston who came highly recommended by Ed Rooney. Her short, iron-gray hair matched the shapeless suit she wore and her glasses were perpetually perched on the end of her long nose.

"Paige, I'm going to confess to the crime," Margo said in a low voice beside her.

"Mother, that's crazy!" Paige said in a hoarse whisper. One night spent in jail was more than enough for her. How had Alex stood it for an entire year? "You haven't done anything wrong."

"I disagree," Margo replied. "I'm the one who brought Stanley into our lives and look where we are today. I won't let you go to jail, Paige. I'd rather take the rap for everything and let the chips fall where they may."

"We are not going to jail," she said. "Rina said the

prosecution's case is flimsy at best, their only real evidence based on the word of a known bigamist and con artist."

"She also said it will probably go to trial." Margo squared her shoulders. "I don't want you to go through that, Paige. You've got a wonderful life with Alex to look forward to. I want to help make that happen."

"It will happen," she said firmly. "And not by your sacrificing yourself on the altar of motherhood. At least wait and see what happens at the hearing."

"All right," Margo said with a sigh. "But if worse comes to worst…"

"It won't," Paige declared, willing herself to believe it.

Margo turned around to talk with Ed, who sat directly behind them in the front row of the gallery. Paige forced herself not to look around for Alex again. If he was coming, he would have been here by now. The hearing was already running late.

Rina walked over to the table and sat down. "The judge is just about ready to start. Now don't be nervous. This is a routine hearing where the assistant district attorney puts on a miniversion of his case against you. I can cross-examine any of the witnesses that he calls. But I do want to warn you that Mr. Stanislawski will be one of them."

"What about us?" Paige asked. "Can we testify?"

Rina hesitated. "That is your right, but I wouldn't

recommend it. Anything you say today can be used against you in the trial."

"So you're certain it will go to trial?" Margo asked.

Rina shrugged. "Nothing is certain. It depends how it goes today. Judge Greene will have to decide if there's a strong suspicion that a crime was committed and that you committed it. If that burden is met, you'll be bound over for trial."

The bailiff called the case and Rina went into full lawyer mode, presenting motions and asking that the case be dismissed for lack of evidence. The judge listened respectfully, but didn't seem inclined to rule in their favor.

Then Stanley was called to the stand.

Paige sensed her mother tensing beside her and reached over to squeeze her hand. Stanley didn't look at Margo or Paige as he took an oath to tell the truth. Then the assistant district attorney, Mr. Welles, began to examine him.

Stanley spun a seamless story that made it seem as if he was the unwitting pawn in some grand conspiracy scheme orchestrated by Paige and her mother. He had dates, names and places all at his fingertips and those fingers were all pointed straight at them.

It seemed to Paige that no one could believe a word out of this man's mouth, yet the judge was leaning forward in his chair, listening intently to Stanley's story.

At last it was time for the cross-examination. Rina stood up and adjusted her glasses. "Tell me, Mr. Weaver... Or should I call you Mr. Stanislawski?"

He smiled. "I answer to both."

"I'm sure you do," Rina replied. "In fact, haven't you used several aliases in your lifetime?"

"A few," he admitted.

"Isn't it a fact, Mr. Stanislawski, that you change your name as often as you change wives and in both cases, not always legally?"

"Is that a question?" Stanley asked, looking over at the judge.

"Perhaps you could rephrase it, counselor," the judge suggested.

"I'll withdraw it, Your Honor." She shuffled some papers on the table in front of her. "So, Mr. Stanislawski, are you telling this court that you never personally approached a client of Bay Bouquets for money or threatened to reveal sensitive information if they didn't comply?"

Stanley leaned toward the microphone in front of him. "All I'm saying is that I was just the flower delivery man. Once I figured out what was really going on there, I began to fear for my safety. That's why I left in the dead of night."

Paige wanted to punch him, but that would hardly impress the judge. Stanley had lined up all his lies so neatly that there seemed to be no way to trip him up. The only person who could possibly do

so was his sister Hildy, and she'd already told Rina
that she refused to testify against her little brother.

"I'm through with this witness, Your Honor,"
Rina said, her voice laced with disgust.

"Any more witnesses, counselor?" the judge
asked the district attorney.

He rose to his feet. "Yes, Your Honor, I'd like to
call Alex Mackopoulos to the stand."

Paige swallowed a gasp of surprise as she turned
toward the back of the courtroom to watch Alex
walk inside. His brother Nico followed behind him,
along with an older woman she guessed to be Thea
Mackopoulos. They sat in the front row near Ed
Rooney while Alex proceeded to the witness stand.

Her palms grew damp as Alex took the oath. *Why
was he testifying for the state?* She tried to read his
mood, but he avoided her gaze, concentrating fully
on the questions put to him by the assistant district
attorney.

"Please state your name and place of employ-
ment."

"Alexander Mackopoulos," he said clearly. "I'm
the full-time financial manager at Mackopoulos Imports and do part-time work at other area businesses."

"You are the son of the late Lucian Mackopoulos?"

"That's right."

"And your father was the victim of blackmail. Is
that correct?"

"Yes. His private conversations were secretly recorded, then we were threatened with the release of the sensitive information contained on the tape."

"Did he receive this threat in person?"

"No," Alex replied. "My father was too ill to realize what was happening. My brother and I received the phone calls at his office, but the voice was always mechanically altered."

"So it could have been a man or a woman?"

"I suppose so," Alex conceded.

Paige sagged back against her chair. So far he wasn't helping her case at all. She wanted him to hold her again. To kiss away all her anxieties and fears. But he seemed remote on the stand, barely looking in her direction.

"What did the caller tell you to do?" Mr. Welles asked.

"Mail the package of money in unmarked bills to a post office on the corner of Third and Rivendale," Alex replied. "The outside of the envelope was to be marked P.O. Box 548."

"Did you and your brother follow through on these instructions?"

"To the letter."

The attorney nodded, marking something down on his yellow legal pad. "And did either of you go to the post office to see who picked up the package?"

"No."

The state's attorney pulled a letter out of his file

folder. "This is an affidavit from the postmaster at the aforementioned post office. The box is registered in the name of Margo Weaver."

Paige glanced at her mother, who had gone very pale. She herself was numb, just waiting to wake up from this horrible dream.

The judge perused the affidavit, then handed it to Rina for her to review.

The state's attorney leaned his forearms on the podium in front of him, looking more confident in his case by the second. "Tell us, Mr. Mackopoulos, did you ever discover how your father's conversations had been recorded?"

"Yes, we hired a security firm to conduct a thorough search of his office and they found a recording device buried in one of the plants leased to our company by Bay Bouquets."

The state's attorney smiled. "Thank you. No more questions."

Paige stared straight ahead. Alex had just unwittingly bolstered the state's case against them. Or maybe he'd done it on purpose in some arrangement with the prosecutor to protect his family secret. She didn't really believe it, but everything seemed surreal to her at this moment.

Paige's lawyer rose to her feet to begin the cross-examination. "Mr. Mackopoulos, did you become romantically involved with Paige Hanover a year ago to investigate whether or not she was involved in this alleged blackmail scheme?"

"Yes, I did."

The assistant district attorney looked up, as if he was surprised by this information.

"And what did you discover?"

"That she's completely innocent."

"Objection." Mr. Welles rose to his feet. "Calls for speculation."

"Sustained," the judge said.

"Do you believe her mother is guilty of this alleged crime?"

"Same objection," the state's attorney called out.

"Sustained," said the judge. "Move on, counselor."

Rina moved closer to the witness stand. "Are you in love with Paige Hanover?"

For the first time, Alex met her gaze and the warmth she saw in his eyes gave her hope. "Yes. I'm very much in love with her."

She could hear the state's attorney groan under his breath, but he didn't object.

"Then can you tell us why you are testifying for the state?"

"Because this is supposed to be a search for the truth," Alex replied. "And I have a videotape and another witness that proves Paige and her mother didn't do anything wrong."

"Objection," screeched the state's attorney.

The judge held up one hand, then turned to Rina Halpern. "What's on this tape?"

"I have no idea, Your Honor. This is the first I've heard of it."

The judge looked at Mr. Welles, who tossed his pencil onto the table in front of him. "I don't know either, Your Honor. Mr. Mackopoulos conveniently neglected to inform me about this during our brief meeting."

"Mr. Mackopoulos," the judge said at last. "Can you describe the contents of this videotape?"

"It's a recording of my father's memorial service. Stanley Weaver, or Wally Stanislawski, appears on this tape in conversation with my mother after the ceremony. He's offering to sell her the blackmail tapes he recorded in my father's office."

"Hearsay, Your Honor," the district attorney said. "Also, this videotape has not been authenticated yet."

Rina stood up and motioned to Thea and Nico Mackopoulos seated in the gallery. "We have what I assume are members of the Mackopoulos family to verify the tape."

Paige held her breath as the judge weighed his options. At last he said, "I'll allow it."

Thea pulled the tape out of her bag and handed it to Rina, who slipped it into the television VCR on a metal stand in the corner.

The courtroom was silent as the tape was fast-forwarded to the crucial moment. Stanley Weaver appeared on the screen, speaking with Thea. His hair was a different color, but the resemblance was unmistakable. The microphone on the video recorder had even picked up some of the conversation. Enough to prove that Stanley had just lied on the stand when he'd claimed that he'd never approached anyone for money in exchange for secretly recorded tapes.

Then the television screen went blank.

Rina rose slowly to her feet. "Judge, in light of this new evidence, I'd like to renew my motion to dismiss this case on lack of evidence. It's clear that this tape has completely invalidated Stanislawski's sworn testimony on the witness stand, which is the foundation for the case against my clients."

Judge Greene arched a silver eyebrow as he looked at the assistant district attorney. "Well?"

Paige watched the prosecutor slowly rise to his feet, as if debating the arguments against the motion in his mind.

But instead of objecting, he did just the opposite. "The state would like to withdraw the charges against Paige Hanover and Margo Weaver."

"Good decision," Judge Greene said, then smiled at them. "You ladies are free to go."

They both just sat there for a moment, too stunned to react. Then Margo reached out and hugged her daughter, a sob of relief clogging in her throat.

"Paige," Alex said, standing directly behind her.

She turned and flew into his arms. "It's over, Alex. It's finally over."

"The bad part's over," Alex said. "The good part is just beginning." Then he kissed her and Paige knew she was truly free. Free to love him without doubts or worry or fear.

"Then let's start with our wedding," she replied. "I'm thinking May."

He frowned. "Next May? That's over a year away."

"The last day of this May," she informed him. "As in two weeks from now."

"You can't possibly plan a wedding all by yourself in two weeks."

"I won't be planning it by myself," she countered. "My mother and your mother will help me."

"That's right," Thea said, interjecting herself into their conversation. "I can bake the wedding cake and fix all the Greek food."

"See?" Paige said. "And my mother can arrange the flowers and prepare the invitations."

Alex turned to see Margo all wrapped up in Ed Rooney's arms. "It looks like your mother will have her hands full planning her own wedding before too long."

"Then Paige and I will take care of everything on our own," Thea declared.

"That's crazy," Nico said, joining the conversation. "The stress will be too much for you, Mom."

Alex turned to Paige. "And you have a business to run and college classes at night. It just won't work."

"It will work," Paige affirmed, exchanging a smile with her future mother-in-law. She already felt like part of the family.

"That's right," Thea said. "Because the Mackopoulos women are strong enough to handle anything."

_____Epilogue_____

FRANCO SAT in the foyer of the apartment house and booted up his new laptop computer. He was ready to begin his masterpiece, flexing his fingers to prepare them for a marathon writing session.

The skirt had worked its magic once again, reuniting Paige and Alex. They didn't realize the skirt was the key, of course, but Franco knew the truth. And now he was going to immortalize it on the silver screen.

He laid all his notes out around him, then stared at the blank computer screen, waiting for inspiration to hit. What he needed was the perfect opening line. Something to grab his audience by the throat and never let go.

Unfortunately, Franco couldn't think of anything scintillating at the moment. He was tired from his karate class, and the enchilada he'd grabbed on the way home had given him heartburn. A great writer couldn't work with heartburn.

So instead he clicked on the solitaire game that came free with his computer and began to play. The repetitive activity would free his subconscious to come up with something really creative.

Three hours later, Franco forced himself to click off the solitaire game and close his laptop computer. A man could get addicted to something like that if he wasn't careful. Fortunately, Franco had a lot of self-discipline.

He glanced at the clock on the wall, realizing with a start that his favorite show was almost on. Turning his chair around, he leaned forward and switched on the set, the theme music already starting.

"Welcome to another addition of *UFO Watch*," exclaimed the breathless announcer. "Tonight we bring you a special follow-up story featuring two women who lost their men under suspicious circumstances. Some call it a bizarre alien abduction, but this mother-daughter duo call it Fate of cosmic proportions."

Franco sat up as a wedding photo of Alex and Paige flashed on the screen, along with a candid shot of a woman he recognized as Paige's mother dancing cheek-to-cheek with an older gentleman.

"That's right, boys and girls," the announcer exclaimed. "The Left-Behind Bride decided to leave her single days behind when she married the man of her cosmic dreams. Her mother has found true love again as well with a man who shares her avid interests in UFOs."

"So join us as we explore a new segment to our

program," the announcer said, breathless with excitement. "We're calling it 'Matchmakers In The Sky.'"

Franco smiled to himself as he turned off the television set and grabbed his laptop. He finally had the perfect idea for a high-concept screenplay. An alien-earthling quadrangle, featuring the skirt that brought them all together.

It would be out of this world.

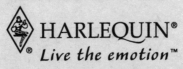

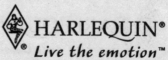

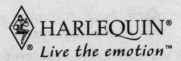

If you enjoyed what you just read,
then we've got an offer you can't resist!

Take 2 bestselling
love stories FREE!

Plus get a FREE surprise gift!

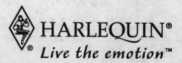

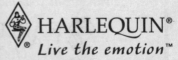

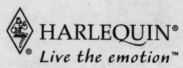